SUMMER MURPHY

A. J. GENIS

MOUNTAIN ARBOR
PRESS

MOUNTAIN ARBOR
PRESS *an imprint of BookLogix*

Alpharetta, GA

Copyright © 2019 by A. J. Genis

All rights reserved. No part of this book may be reproduced or transmitted in any form or by any means, electronic or mechanical, including photocopying, recording, or any information storage and retrieval system, without permission in writing from the author.

ISBN: 978-1-63183-508-7 - Paperback
eISBN: 978-1-63183-509-4 - ePub
eISBN: 978-1-63183-510-0 - mobi

Library of Congress Control Number: 2019905130

Printed in the United States of America   0 8 1 5 1 9

♾ This paper meets the requirements of ANSI/NISO Z39.48-1992 (Permanence of Paper)

Gracias to the dictionary, Staples,
and the Santa Barbara Mission,
where I get solace and inspiration.

Life is what happens to you while you're busy making other plans.

Chapter One

1992

The mourners poured in throughout the afternoon, delivering offerings—sweets, meats of all kinds, and home-baked cakes and breads to feast on. Volunteers took care of the kitchen and bar duty. They all came with heavy hearts, knowing the irony that this was to have been Major Brendon Murphy's last mission. It had become a terrible reality.

Murphy had been one of the space program's finest pilots—the second astronaut to have broken the sound barrier. It was unthinkable to call this an accidental death.

Laughter and tears contributed to the day. There was an undertone of disbelief in the softly spoken words. Children moved silently about, with somber faces. Summer Murphy, Brendon's daughter, heard whispered within the crowd, over and over, "It's so awful, just awful, it just can't be. I still can't believe he's gone," always accompanied by a shiver and a shake of their heads. Brendon Murphy's bereavement picture was one of a man in robust health. That was how they would always choose to remember him.

Major Ed Ryan and his wife, Mary, opened their home to those wishing to pay their respects. Both military personnel and private citizens at Edwards Air Force Base came by the dozens, filling the small house and yard to overflowing.

In the tradition of a true Irish wake, there was something of a raucous crowd hoisting a few to honor the man they had always admired, while recounting endless stories about their fallen hero. No one attending really believed Murphy's crash had been pilot error; he was the most skilled pilot there ever was.

Summer Murphy came from her home on the base to hear the accolades paid her dad. Her grief was so deep it was difficult to hear him eulogized so intimately. The obituary column had used such a very young picture. That she could not ever remember him that young was startling to her. Summer had been so young when her mother disappeared that she had not one solid memory of her. She had been not yet three years old.

Father and daughter had always been inseparable. Brendon spent every moment he could with Summer. He brought her up to be an independent person. Everyone who knew them marveled at the devotion and care a career officer could give to his child. He never considered remarrying.

Those old-timers who could remember her mother thought Summer grew up to be a carbon copy of Dawn Murphy, the same sensuous mouth, high cheekbones, green eyes, natural blond, wavy hair, and a tall, willowy figure. Yes, a spitting image of Dawn Murphy.

There were no pictures to give her daughter a memory of her beautiful mother. Brendon had been bitter, and hurt. And he made sure there were none.

As a child, Summer had been cared for by several of the wives on the base, like Mary Ryan, who had loved and fussed over her. They would all try to comfort her now. She would have no lacking for motherly love. But deep down in her heart, Summer yearned to know the woman who had given birth to her.

Summer sat down next to Ed Ryan, who said for lack of anything better to say, "You look as if you need to eat something, my darling girl." He repeated himself, conscious of the pain and sorrow she must be feeling.

Mary scolded him, and shushed him away. "Hush, Ed, now leave the girl alone." Knowing Mary had Summer in hand, he considerately moved away.

Mary Ryan took the grief-stricken girl into her arms, swaying back and forth as if she were rocking a child.

"Your father knew you'd make him proud." Mary's voice was strained from crying throughout that day. With a quavering voice, she added, "Summer, I know you will have success in your chosen field. We've always known that since you were a small girl. I remember all the poems and stories you wrote. I kept not a few, but dozens of them." Mary gave her a quick hug and patted her back, much too emotional to continue.

In the late afternoon, long after most of the guests left, Mary told her, "Your mother wrote poetry too." She slipped a sheaf of papers into Summer's hands, in a conspiratorial way.

"There is one more thing you need to do. Your dad made a will. Legal is holding it now for you, sweet girl. Go there. But before you leave, promise me," Mary coaxed.

"I'll take care of it," Summer assured her with a sad nod of her head. "My bus leaves at eleven tonight. This day has been awful, God awful," she said with a shiver. "I won't be back here for a very long time, Mary."

She turned and quickly walked away, too tired to deal with any more of the mourners.

Chapter Two

Lieutenant Terrence Whitmore, Military Legal Counsel, was a stoic man with little sympathy to spare. His conceit was clearly telegraphed by his demeanor and a chest covered in medals. What few hairs he had were foolishly combed over slick on his bald head.

Summer sat in the chair he'd gestured for her to take, opposite his desk. She noticed his name bar on the desk. He had additional plaques with his name all around the small office. Her habit as a writer was to observe the minutiae. Summer was uncomfortable and wished the ordeal to hear about her dad's will were over.

She sat for what seemed like a long time in silence.

The lawyer neither smiled nor offered her any sympathy. He talked at her rather than to her. Never once did he mention the unusual loss of her father.

After five minutes, he picked up a sheath of papers from his cluttered desktop and went through them page by page. When he was finished, he spoke to her in a dictatorial tone as if she were not right there, as he lectured, "Long as you're willing to manage your money carefully, not engage in highflyers, you should be all right, Miss Murphy. Now sign right here." He offered her a pen, directing her to sign where he had made an X.

"Manage what?" she asked, clueless as to what this was all about.

He ignored her question and carefully picked up the documents from the desk, again pointing at the place for a signature.

Summer was confused. "Sign for what?"

"Your father left you a savings of $125,000 in a bank account, and a military insurance policy in the amount of $125,000. This gives you quite a nice nest egg." He smiled at her for the first time. "A tidy sum, Miss."

"Oh my god," Summer gasped. "My dad never discussed annuities, insurance, or dying."

Dying had definitely been out of the question. Her dad had been invincible, or so she liked to think. This was more money than she had ever thought to have. She found it difficult to wrap her mind around it. The need to escape was choking her.

Summer answered brusquely, "I have a bus to catch, just show me where to sign!" She bolted from that office, feeling her father's spirit close. It wrapped her in a cloak of tranquility.

Leaving the desert was in turn both painful and bittersweet. She would be beginning the rest of her life. Living without her father, her staunchest ally, seemed unthinkable. It had always been just the two of them against the world.

Now she must accept that her father was gone. Her inheritance would always be the instrument to remind her of just how much he had worried about her and loved her. His death cut her like a rusty razor.

Summer left on a Greyhound bus just before midnight to start her new life in Los Angeles. She took a seat and prayed no one would sit beside her. She was bone tired from the many well-wishers who had known and admired her father. She only wanted to sleep and wake up far from grief until she arrived in LA.

Brendon Murphy's blessings echoed like a mantra in her head, over and over as the bus wheels churned over the highway. Summer closed her eyes and his voice spoke to her in a dream. Her father's voice in her head sounded as real as if he were there beside her:

Write from your heart, love. Remember, Irish women were warriors in Ireland, he emphasized, *and you don't take crap from anyone. You hear what I'm saying?*

The drone of the bus motor and her dad's comforting words lulled her to an exhausted sleep. She curled up to the window, her coat bundled up against the cold night air on the frigid window. Summer slept for the long ride to Los Angeles.

Chapter Three

In the rush of registering at the American Film Institute, Summer had completely forgotten to inquire about a place to live. When arriving in LA, she had simply checked into a cheap motel on Sunset Boulevard. Luckily a woman in the registrar's office, a Mrs. Lee, recommended a place a stone's throw from the Institute. Mrs. Lee was a petite, kindly woman who touted the Jones Boardinghouse to be a safe place. She went on and on about it.

"That Mrs. Jones's a character," she said. "She takes people in, you know, in the business." She reiterated, "Been doing it since her husband died fifteen years ago. They were career extras, don't ya know, deary. They worked steady. Good show-biz people with big hearts. You try her first, hon. If you're lucky she'll have a room for you."

Mrs. Lee was rapidly scribbling the address on a notepad and putting it gently into Summer's hand.

* * *

The next day, Summer walked over to Mrs. Jones' home carrying her small suitcase. The boardinghouse looked exactly how Mrs. Lee described it—an old stone and wooden California bungalow with a wrap-around front porch, just ten blocks from the Film Institute.

Unlike most properties on Western Avenue, Mrs. Jones' place looked freshly painted, with a garden neatly tended. Rose bushes lined either side of the walkway up to the porch of the house, which was un-usual because flowers don't grow too well in the de-sert. The house was a jewel in the middle of the squalor of Western Avenue, even walking distance to the Film Institute.

Ever optimistic, Summer placed her suitcase against the wall of the house beside the door and rang the doorbell. Not a moment later, Emma Jones opened the door, smiling wide at the pretty young girl. Her vivid red hair was pinned with fresh flowers, and her face seemed surprisingly youthful for a woman of un-determined age.

Summer started to explain why she was there. "Mrs. Lee at the—"

"I know, I know, Harriet Lee from AFI told you about a room." She waved the girl silent, then kept waving her into the house. "Come on, come on, I don't have all day. Follow me, I do have one room to rent."

Mrs. Jones bounded the stairs two at a time. At the top of the landing, she flung open a door to a room, then said, "I personally couldn't live in anything so small as this, Missy. Want to think about it, or should I hold it?"

"No, no, it will be just fine," Summer protested emphatically, determined to have this room. She needed to vacate the Palm Motel no matter what!

She insisted, "I'm used to small rooms." The room really could have been a walk-in closet. It had a bed and a few mismatched pieces of furniture. Faded floral wallpaper covered the walls. But, it was surprisingly charming.

Summer saw it as a challenge—she was good at fixing things up. "I'd like it. For sure. I can do things to make it cozy." She already had ideas spinning.

"It's already cozy, right?" Mrs. Jones joked about the size of the room. "Hon, you can do anything you like in here to doll it up, except paint the walls black."

Summer reassured her, "Oh, no! I wouldn't do anything like that." She smiled wide, showing the landlady her sincerity. "Mrs. Lee was so nice to tell me—"

Emma Jones, as if remembering a nasty memory, said, "I had a hippie once who, no kidding, painted his room black. It's all yours, sweetheart. Move in anytime. Seventy-five dollars a month and you get two meals a day. Choose which. Most like breakfast and dinner. You can move in soon as you want."

"Would right now be too soon? I have my suitcase on the porch."

Mrs. Jones laughed. "No kidding?" She liked this

girl on sight. She was pretty enough to be an actress with her fresh-scrubbed looks and sunny disposition. She'd be nice to have around.

"It's all yours, young lady. When meals are served is tacked up right on the back of your closet door." She opened the small closet and pointed as she handed Summer the key she plucked from her pocket. With the two of them in the room, it was crowded.

* * *

At dinner that night, Summer found she was the only boarder who was a student. Everyone else appeared to be gainfully employed. Most were involved in some form of show business, and that pleased her.

Of the tenants at dinner she met that first night was Cheryl Lane, a costume designer. She was maybe twenty-five. Her outfit was a crazy quilt of colors and patterns Summer had only seen in fashion magazines. Her hair was streaked with colors to match her outfit. Jerry Simon, a writer, was employed by Disney Studios, writing one-sheets for Disney.

He explained when she looked quizzical. "Movie posters. We have to tell the whole plot in one line. So we come up with catchy phrases. Sells the movie. One-sheets." He wore his blond hair slicked back with a twinkle in the bluest of eyes. And very sincere eyes they were, with a hint of blue mascara surrounding them. He had a slight build, dressed in boyish clothes that made him look like a clipped-out Old Navy ad. He made it clear he would love to help her to settle in.

Within days, Summer realized Hollywood Boulevard's glamour she had dreamt of all her life was just a thing of the past. The begrimed streets were laden with T-shirt shops and tawdry souvenir shops. Crime and drugs were rampant. This was the ex-glamour capital of the world. The Walk of Fame laid out on the streets in brass was the only thing to remind her of Hollywood's glory days. Unfortunately, all that was left of Hollywood were derelict streets.

She would have cried if she weren't so excited to begin her career. Still, Summer ventured out to see the famous Hollywood tourist attractions. She visited the Grauman's Chinese Theatre, where footprints and handprints were imprinted in cement alongside the signature of major stars. The stars signed their names in the cement of the courtyard, making it the busiest tourist spot on the boulevard. A few blocks to the east was the Egyptian Theatre, its courtyard the mirror image of a Cecil B. DeMille film. Midway down Hollywood Boulevard was the restaurant Musso & Frank, where the waiters looked as if they were from Central Casting. Summer had coffee at the famous Hollywood Roosevelt Hotel, where the lobby was decorated as if it were 1929, all in dark shades of rich mahogany wood and burnished leather upholstered furniture.

There were numerous places advertised in the

handout from the Chamber of Commerce to visit, no charge. One especially unusual one was the cemetery smack in the middle of Hollywood, next to the Paramount Pictures film studio.

Summer longed for the memory of her father's encouragement and missed so many little things, mostly confiding in him. The scent of his sweet tobacco as he smoked his pipe, and the sound of him tapping it against the tabletop as he filled it, had always told her he was near. Those first nights at the boardinghouse, Summer wept bitter tears, tears that had been bottled up in her soul since the wake. She had so much to do getting settled that she had not mourned properly.

The facts of his crash were unfortunately inconclusive. She might never have closure.

* * *

The pounding of pile-driving equipment boring into concrete for the new subway system and the knocking at her door woke her from her exhausted sleep. Summer glanced at her watch—it was eight o'clock in the morning. She was averaging about three hours a night with all the unfamiliar sounds of the city. Oddly enough, she awoke feeling better than she had for days.

Throwing on a terry robe and tying it at her waist, she quickly opened the door to find Mrs. Jones standing there with a large glass of orange juice and her look-see eyes wide open. Curiosity was written all over Mrs. Jones' face as she sized up the young woman.

"Miss Murphy, you missed breakfast twice this week. Comes with the room, ya know. Seven to nine o'clock a.m. is what's posted." She tapped her watch to verify. "Most of my guests leave before eight in the morning. I thought you might need a good start. Writers need food for their brain. Fresh squeezed," she bragged, pushing a large glass of orange juice at Summer. "You know, we have six orange trees in my garden and one lemon," she continued, all the while assessing the room Summer occupied, which was neat as a pin.

"You shouldn't have, Mrs. Jones." Summer was flustered, embarrassed to have this kind of attention.

"No big deal, being your first week at the Institute and all." Emma Jones was noticeably embarrassed herself to have been caught doing something nice. "Here!" She thrust the glass of juice at Summer. "Take it!"

"Thank you," Summer said. "I'll try to be on time for meals, or call if I can't make it." She tried to show her appreciation for the stoic woman's gesture of kindness. She cast her eyes downward, sure her eyes were red from crying. The last thing she wanted to do was to explain her tears to a stranger.

Hiding a little behind the door, Summer forced a smile and waited for the woman to decide to leave. "Thanks again for the juice," she said sweetly, moving her door an inch or two shut with each word.

"No problem," Mrs. Jones said, giving her a practiced half-grin, and she turned and went quickly downstairs.

Emma Jones had noticed the girl's reddened eyes. Summer had radiated an underlying sadness since the first day she came and took the place. Emma had wondered at first sight if the beautiful young girl was even old enough to be in the grant program at AFI.

Summer had been dressed simply in a short skirt, white T-shirt, and tennis shoes. Remarkably, the young girl wore no visible makeup. Most of the kids today slathered that junk on. Emma thought this girl had class written all over her, like she could be a headliner. She understood Summer was already working on a script of her own. Her friend Mrs. Lee had filled in all the blanks. Emma thought her a welcome addition to the house.

Chapter Four

In the weeks that followed, Jerry Simon almost always knocked on Summer's door every morning, shouting, "I'm going over the hill to Burbank, babycakes. I can drive you to the Tute—it's on my way, ya know."

"Give me a few minutes more," Summer usually called out while she made her bed and dressed quickly. Then she flew down the stairs two at a time to run out the door, rush down the walkway, and climb into his classic yellow Volkswagen. It was an antique, she guessed, maybe as much as thirty years old?

Jerry smiled. "It's a sunny day. I'll put the top down, if it won't blow your do?" He was as chivalrous as a knight of yore. Jerry gossiped nonstop the half-dozen blocks it took to reach the Film Institute.

"If you want to know who's sleeping with who, just ask me," Jerry said. "I know people who know people." He looked smug. His falsetto voice, speed-talking, and gestures made the gossip fun.

When Summer exited his car one morning, she

leaned over to press a kiss to his clean-shaven check. She caught a glimpse of a blush on his cute face as he pulled away.

* * *

She ran up the steps of the Institute. She was late for her appointment with Solley Lester. The professor, Solley, had inherited the only office space available at the American Film Institute when he had offered to teach two years ago. The windows of that room were still painted black. So many years ago, to help the war effort during World War II, the Sisters of the Immaculate Heart Convent had blackened all of the outside street-side windows. The former owners of the campus, patriotic nuns, had left them in that condition after the war ended.

Solley Lester rather liked the inquisition touch. The seventy-five-year-old curmudgeon was one of the legendary literary agents in show business. He drove his students mercilessly. To his delight, he knew it helped make them dig deeper. The students liked to call him Herr Professor.

Solley Lester never tired of looking at Summer Murphy's beautiful face. She was a ray of sunshine in the class. He raised his eyes above his Ben Franklin glasses to be sure she was sufficiently uncomfortable while he marked her manuscript up. Summer sat in the wooden folding chair across from his desk. They were having a one-on-one today, as he did with all students who submitted their papers on time.

"Any work submitted and on my desk by Tuesday will be read," he'd bellowed. "One day past—TOO LATE!" He added, "Trying negates doing!"

Surprisingly he shouted loud enough to be heard two rooms over. He had a mountain of smash hits to his credit over six decades.

Summer had been left with a clutching fear in the ensuing weeks that she wouldn't measure up to his high standards. Her classmates were some of the best potential screenwriters, chosen from worldwide submissions to come and study at the Film Institute. It was likely the talent to produce scripts for the new millennium would come out of this group.

Not being good enough, not measuring up, was always the theme for Summer Murphy's panic. Fear was a trait unlike her, but fearful she was. Solley felt it was in their best interests to prepare writers for the real world, where a cup of kindness was rare. He did anything he could to bedevil the fledgling screenwriters.

Summer had written and rewritten enough pages for five screenplays in an effort to please him. She'd made Solley Lester the new approval figure in her life now. She craved his approval to the point of exhaustion.

Solley picked up her script to make his point. "Hear me, Summer, kid, you got bupkes, nada, nothing, not enough. You're not digging deep enough. You've got to put more meat into your story."

Summer looked whipped. She didn't understand exactly what he was saying, for the moment.

Solley liked to stick it to them, to let the students suffer. He knew water would seek its own level. The real writers would eventually surface. He leaned back in his chair, happy to observe her discomfort.

Sitting in this dreadful room the past half hour felt like an eternity to Summer. Time seemed to stand still as she watched him read and reread passages of her work, constantly running his hand over the top of his bald pate, creating its high sheen. In actuality, only ten minutes had passed since looking at her watch for the tenth time. The students all referred to Solley's small excuse for an office as "the dungeon." Now it was Summer's turn on the rack.

Summer counted the sacrifices she had made these past few months. Bartending was the biggest thing. It was such good money. She was determined not to touch her inheritance. Living the life of a cloistered nun was for the birds, but it didn't do her any good to dwell on that. Writing was her mission. Sitting on the edge of her seat, she held her breath and gritted her teeth.

They called it killer luck to have the opportunity to study screenwriting with Solley Lester. The short, compact man was considered a giant in show business. Summer had heard Solley was known to give writers ulcers, while at his advanced age he had already outlived most of his contemporaries. He seemed to enjoy excellent health himself.

Summer had never had a nerve in her body until she met Solley. Now she was all uptight. Solley looked up at the girl he'd come to admire for her persistence, her talent, her manner, and her beauty. She was outspoken and assured in a proud way. Not too many people seemed to get close to her. If the men in his class flirted with her, Summer's green eyes would flash, aloof without disdain, letting anyone know she was interested only in her work.

This young woman had a rare and beguiling mystique. Most importantly, the girl wrote the best stuff he'd seen in a long time. He thought she could be the next-best thing to chopped liver.

Solley had a nose for spotting a superstar in the making, or recycling a stalled one. He read that in her writing. He set her manuscript down like precious porcelain, rubbing his hands together as if for warmth. He gave her a look she couldn't interpret, then wiped his glasses and averted his eyes. He took in a deep breath, filling his lungs. He was stalling for time, and he was good at pregnant pauses.

Summer's skin began to crawl. "Mr. Lester . . . say something, please!"

He scratched his ear, and said incredulously, his

delivery accusatory, "A man and woman, pirates in the eighteenth century, a love story that burns up the paper it's written on. This is not the average bodice ripper. It has all of the earmarks of a 'Tom Jones.' SPICY!"

Solley slid his eyes up to the heavens, then gave her a sidelong glance of disbelief. He shook his head. "Summer Murphy, I think I know you . . . or I would almost suspect plagiarism. What do you kids say? Totally awesome?"

Summer was on the defensive. Her eyes glistened with emotion as she glared at him, not willing to believe this.

He smiled wide, hoping to take the edge off. You could almost cut the tension with a knife. "I'm not accusing you, so take that look off your face."

"Give me a break! The woman in my story was fashioned after a real pirate. Grania, the Irish called her, She-King. She lived centuries ago, I read books and books about her. Flesh and blood characters are what I used to mold my story."

"Oh, research is good!" Solley agreed.

"This is a Valium moment for me, Solley. I want the skinny. Did you like it or not?"

Branded by the press as "the man who shoots from the lips," Solley was reduced to answering, "I found it satisfying."

"Satisfying?" Summer was incredulous. "Just what

does that mean? Is that a way of saying thanks, but no thanks?"

"Let me lay this out for you. Your story has great action scenes. Special effects have become the hidden star in films, and there are plenty of those in your story. That's a plus, the love story is remarkable, and—" He bit his lower lip while thinking. "Someone will produce a swashbuckler! The time is ripe for pirate stories that might make money. They haven't made one in a long time."

"Great, I've at least picked the right genre," Summer said. She was clearly excited. "That's reassuring!" She sat back down and looked boldly into his eyes, looking for answers. "Well?"

Summer had an independent air, but Solley could see her soft side. "You have a great love story here also." His faded blue eyes held a depth of sincerity. "There's always a but, my dear, so get used to it. Your script needs rewrites!"

He raised his eyebrows and splayed his hands palms up, waiting for her reaction.

"Really?" she said in a small, wondrous whisper. "How much of it needs to be rewritten?"

"All, all of it. For a shiksa you catch on slow. But it is good, really good, and you'll see it will be even better."

No amount of control could hold back the foolish grin that spread over her face.

"You're kidding . . . right?" She was restraining the desire to scream wildly and jump up and down.

"No, on the emmis, it's good. Damn good!" Solley answered with a straight face.

Something in Summer's attitude right now made him remember the first day he'd met her. Actress and director Lee Grant had brought her to meet him. The girl absolutely lit up his gloomy office that day. Her graceful posture and breathtaking looks captivated him immediately.

Seeing his reaction, Lee Grant said to him, "You're old, Solley, but definitely not dead." She had a good laugh at his expense. He clearly appreciated a beautiful woman. "Miss Murphy," she said, "looks like you're in good hands."

With her body half in/half out of the doorway, Lee Grant added, "Solley, if the kid can't write, send her to me. I'm always directing and casting something. We could teach her to act. With a face like hers, the camera's got to love her." Before Solley could answer, Lee Grant made an actor's quick exit.

Solley shook off the memory to get back to the business at hand. "Miss Murphy, it is one of the best first drafts I've seen in a long time." He smiled at her like a proud parent. She looked up at him with her haunting green eyes and a genuine smile the Irish wrote love songs about. That smile told him she was all right. She could handle what it took to be a great screenwriter.

"Why write about pirates?" he asked, giving her a sly look.

She wasted no time answering him. "I was a kid with not a hell of a lot to do out there at Edwards Air Force Base, besides chasing tumbleweeds. Mostly we watched pictures from the thirties and forties." Summer continued, "I saw some movies a dozen of times or more. My escape. You could say I had movies in place of playmates."

Sensing her need to talk it out, he didn't interrupt. He wanted to let her reveal a small sliver of her life story.

"I loved the big technicolor swashbucklers. Matter of fact, all period pictures. I read all I could about pirates and then discovered there were also hundreds of women who went to sea to became pirates themselves.

"The romance, adventure, the color, the . . ." She drew a deep breath, and then continued. "My father was one of those brave men in the space program, a daredevil test pilot. Not unlike the privateers and the pirates who went into uncharted territories centuries ago. Air Force fly-jocks—as a matter of fact, they call themselves bandits, or pirates." Her demeanor had changed with the mention of her father.

Solley caught her excitement and ran with it. "Ticket buyers better get ready for chivalry and dueling pistols. I believe in evolution. This film could be a love poem to that period of pirates and heavy bosoms. I know some actresses who will give their eyeteeth for such a part.

You cover social causes that are current today, women's rights, individual human rights." Solley broke the mood by asking her half in jest, "The way you wrote these sex scenes, Summer. Would it be firsthand experience? Or is it just a wonderful fantasy life?"

Summer answered dryly, "Does it surprise you I know enough about sex to write about it? This is the nineties, after all."

As usual Summer was noncommittal, but she fed fuel to the fire. "I wasn't writing fade-out/fade-in with the rustle of trees," she said with confidence. "I think love scenes can be poetic."

He grinned triumphantly. "These sex scenes are so beautifully crafted. You'll get no red line there." He looked at her wistfully. "I want to pitch your story." He felt the rush of selling a property of this scope again. He tried to look as nonchalant as he could. He said sympathetically, "Say goodbye to your idyllic life, bubala, from here on in it's crazy time. Welcome to the Hollywood I know and love so well. For this weekend, forget about work. Relax, Summer, call family. The worst is yet to come."

"I know it won't be a waltz in the park, Solley. As for family, my dad passed away recently, and I don't know where my mother is. I haven't seen her since I was a baby." Summer had an independent air, but Solley could see disclosing that much was painful. "It's just me."

Solley caught the croak in her voice. There was an uncomfortable moment as he realized she had never mentioned her parents before. He was taken aback. He smiled in sympathy and thought it must be hard for her to confide in him. The girl was so guarded.

"Summer, forgive me, dear. I didn't know," he apologized. "I'm so sorry."

"How could you have known? I want to thank you, Solley."

"For what?"

"This is the first time I have admitted my father is gone to anyone here." Without the slightest feeling of embarrassment, she said, "I'll probably have a job this weekend."

Summer stood, looking serene and confident. She picked up her purse and laid the strap on her shoulder. "I need some time to digest all of this." She gestured at the script that lay on the table between them with a sweep of her arm. "I couldn't possibly concentrate, even if you forced me to."

Solley looked up over his Ben Franklin glasses and closed his eyes, as if to take a catnap. He swiveled the high-back chair around and addressed her with his back to her.

Waving his hand in the air, he said, "Go, go on. Monday we'll get down to the business of turning this dream into a reality."

Summer smiled at the back of his bald head.

Without a doubt, working with him would hit like a nicotine alert, but she counted herself damn lucky to be among the chosen few at AFI singled out for his attention. She bolted from the room without saying goodbye.

Chapter Five

Summer knew by now that Mrs. Jones preferred people to think of her as cold and distant, rather than guess the softhearted person she really was. Jerry Simon became like a girlfriend to her and Mrs. Jones like an aunt. Cheryl Lane got married and moved to Brentwood, but they kept in touch.

Emma couldn't resist talking to Summer about the many wannabes who had passed through her boardinghouse in four decades. Hollywood hopefuls! She considered herself an expert, and after all these years, she could pick the winners. Mrs. Jones told her stories about James Dean, who spent some time as a lodger a few months before he hit it big, back in the fifties. Natalie Wood and Dean were a very hot item then. She would come to pick him up, don't ya know, because he had no transportation. She had a red Thunderbird. She liked to laugh and say, "I got a million of 'em."

Dedication to hard work was the cornerstone of Emma's philosophy. She noticed from the first

Summer's selfless drive. But because she was often a no-show for meals, Emma started saving a bit of dinner for the girl, should she come in late. Emma also took to cutting flowers from her garden and putting a small bouquet in her tiny room. It made her happy doing those small things for her.

Summer shared little of her past. Emma tried her best not to pry, but that was not in her nature. She speculated Summer had suffered some great loss and needed time to heal.

The other renters began to notice a change in the old woman. It was the first time since Henry Jones died that Emma had displayed affection for anyone. The girl had brought out her soft side. Before long, everyone in the boardinghouse was receiving favors from the landlady. Nothing was overt about Emma, who managed to supply little things without fanfare. New curtains or other household items were replaced. It gave a lift to the boarders. Emma Jones gave herself a new perm, wearing her hair in a style still stuck in some faraway decade. Her clothes were now a little more bohemian. In just half a year, the woman's demeanor changed completely.

* * *

On the top of the highboy dresser was a stack of postcards and letters from the Ryans. Summer had been remiss in not answering any of them. Every letter kept her posted on what was going on in their lives and with friends on the base. She promised herself she would get some postcards written, and soon. With every postcard came invitations to visit, but it was too soon to revisit her pain. There still was no conclusion to the fatal accident that had taken her father's life.

Chapter Six

Summer called her girlfriend Loren Palmer from the pay phone in the hall early in the morning after her meeting with Solley Lester. Without a hello, Summer raced on pell-mell: "Hey, I tried to reach you last night. I have some good news and some not-so-good news. Where were you, anyway?"

"Out painting the town scarlet, baby," Loren's silky voice replied.

"You awake yet?" Summer inquired. Not waiting for an answer she pressed on. "Solley liked the script. What do you think of that? There's a possibility he could even get it optioned—after a rewrite. Imagine, Loren!" Summer gushed, breathless.

Loren replied, "You say? I just woke up, baby, what time is it?" She emitted a loud yawn into the receiver, then said, "That's great, babycakes! Mr. Lester's rep is A1, he's a wizard. Literary agents control material, and material is the lifeblood of Hollywood. He is one powerful dude."

"He really is," Summer said, feeling a glow.

"Shoot, girl, pretty soon even your cleaners will know your bank balance." Loren let out a booming laugh, loving her joke. "Everyone will know your name. You'll be tabloid material!"

Between cigarettes and whiskey coupled with late-night partying, Loren's voice was six registers low.

"This whole thing is happening so fast," Summer said. "It's so damn scary. I never craved fame. I just want to write. Am I up for this?"

Loren screamed into the phone, excited for her friend. She let out an explosive guffaw. "'Course you are, girl, 'course you are." She scolded her, "Think about it—you are ready. You have been working your tail off, baby. Mr. Lester doesn't pick losers. Besides, that's what comes with your chosen profession—you good, you get known, they all want to know about you."

"Biggest thrill of my life would be to get my script into development. It's all I can think of now."

Loren intoned in a slow, sexy voice, "Twirl with it, baby. What you worried 'bout? In Hollywood, we say butter up the big guys. You dig?"

Summer laughed to think what her friend implied. One of the boarders moved past her in the narrow hall-way. They exchanged polite smiles. She stepped closer to the pay phone on the wall and in a quieter voice asked if Loren could hear her.

Loren replied, sleep deprived, "Uh-*huh*."

"I'm selling a script, Loren, not myself."

Loren was now fully awake and getting more serious. She lectured, "Miss Murphy, haven't you looked in the mirror lately? You're a babe, a dish, dynamite. I ain't joking. Use it, doll. You go into every meeting with ammunition."

"I'm just worried and scared witless," Summer said. "My whole life hinges on how good my rewrite is." She heaved a loud sigh.

"Writers always have to rewrite, it's a cardinal rule. Go, be a writer." Loren could be heard lighting up a cigarette, inhaling deeply, and blowing a puff of smoke.

Summer laughed. Loren could solve everybody's problems but her own. She also understood why. Loren had a famous father.

Loren said, "Matter of fact, baby, there's a medium I know who for a hundred dollars can fill in your blanks. Like, will you sell this script, to who, and for how much. How 'bout it?" She emitted another loud yawn in Summer's ear. Nine in the morning was the middle of the night to Loren.

"Are you kidding?" Summer asked. "With an extra hundred dollars, I'd spend it on paper for my printer."

"Aw, babycakes, you always crying 'bout the buck." Loren let out a low moan. "I can loan you some green if you need it." Always generous, Loren was totally spontaneous. "My daddy's royalties on his records keep pouring in like vintage wine. Now, Solley Lester is your fairy godfather. You got collateral. So if you're tap city . . . I'll spring. You're a good bet."

Emma noticed Summer hugging the wall in the narrow upper hallway with the phone to her ear. Emma pushed past her with her arms full of linens.

Summer lowered her voice. "You know I'm not much for California metaphysical experiences," she whispered into the receiver. "I appreciate the offer. I'm not broke."

"So why do you live like Cinderella in the attic, baby?" Loren couldn't help giggling with glee.

"I'm frugal," Summer said defensively.

"Girl, you are cheap, cheap, cheap. Face it. I bet you strike it rich and you the only one who doesn't know it." Loren couldn't resist a squeal and one more giggle on the truth.

Summer laughed. She needed to say goodbye, or she would be running late again for her 10:30 appointment with Solley Lester. She confessed, "The dungeon calls. I gotta go. I'll call ya later with an update." To end the conversation she said, "Say good night, Gracie," their little Burns and Allen routine joke.

"Oh, all right, Georgie, good night!" Loren said. "Too bad you don't play around. Wasting all your fine pulchritude, not giving nobody nothing. Come to think of it, being seen with you could ruin a girl's reputation." Loren gave a loud chuckle.

Summer said, "Jeez, Louise, I know I'm difficult." Loren's laughter on the other end was contagious.

"For god's sake, it's not that funny. Bye." Summer laughed to herself, shaking her head as she hung up the phone.

The wall phone rang immediately, and Summer answered. It was for her.

"Summer, Mel Carey." He rambled on pell-mell. "I'm glad I caught you. It's a last-minute thing, babe. I need ya. We booked a party on the Lazzara yacht, and someone with indefinable class like yours who makes tending bar look like ballet is what we need. You know Roger Medvey's seventy-six-foot Lazzara docked in front of the Ritz-Carlton in the marina?"

Mel juggled his usual eight balls. His voice was filled with excitement and anticipation.

"I've read something about it in the newspapers," Summer replied. "Of course I'm interested."

Mel Carey could charm leaves from trees. Loren Palmer, who was on every A-party list in Hollywood, had introduced Summer to him when she first came to town and needed a job. She'd become a regular on their staff. Mel and his brother Steve Carey owned one of the very successful event-planning companies in Hollywood. Over the past year, clients had often asked for Summer specifically to tend bar at their parties.

Not missing a beat, Mel Carey repeated, "The Lazzara yacht is docked out front of the Ritz-Carlton Hotel. In Marina Del Rey. Tomorrow, at six p.m. Can you handle that? What's the story, morning glory?"

Summer said, "Your timing's great, Mel. I'm ready. I have some time off."

Mel's brand of charm made her smile. The brothers had been great to her ever since she first came to Hollywood, making it difficult to refuse them. Summer was also intrigued with the opportunity to see Roger Medvey's glamorous yacht.

"Yes, count me in."

"Yo Mama, congrats!" Mel's voice boomed from the other end. "Roger Medvey's big potatoes, he is right up there with Spielberg and Lucas. Couldn't hurt to know him."

Mel changed his tone and said coyly, "You, like, dropped out. For weeks, and that was making the Carey brothers very sad, girl."

"Well, now I'm back, Mel. My first draft is done," Summer said. She couldn't suppress a grin. "Tending bar relaxes me."

His brother Steve had a crush on her. Mel knew it, and he was just looking out for him. But Summer had only treated them both like her brothers.

* * *

Summer made her 10:30 appointment with Solley

Lester by the skin of her teeth. He proceeded to cut her work to ribbons. At his advanced age, Solley Lester could and did outdistance her in stamina. He was a phenomenon, his focus amazing. He knew what to ax in a script, leaving the best descriptive stuff in place. The legend surrounding him was grounded on a mountain of hits and truth.

"This could be a big-budget movie, my dear." Solley talked as if her deal were set in stone. "We're talking in the neighborhood of a one-hundred-million-dollar budget. Let's give them the goods, a feel-good movie, about triumph of the human spirit. It should be big with the feminists, you know, women's rights, all of that."

His tone was sincere. Solley used honey instead of vinegar to salve her exhaustion, and was always able to get another couple of hours' work out of her before she crashed. He made her stretch as an artist, reaching for goals beyond her imagination. But he exhausted her, always demanding more.

"I suspected you would hang tough, kid," he would say when he cut a section after she had labored on it for days, leaving just a few lines of dialog, knowing a cut of dialog was difficult for the author to take. Slashed with a stroke of his red pencil.

"It's critical you don't get married to every word you write, Summer," he cautioned her over and over. "Remember, sometimes what you leave out of a story is more important than what's left in."

He took pride in giving lessons in filmmaking at every opportunity. It was like he wanted to cram whatever he could, while he could. Moviemaking had been his lifeblood for fifty years.

"You'll see how it works, a collaborative. The director takes over from the writer and they form a sort of partnership." Solley gave her the sheep's-eye glance and a shrug, or some other favorite physical schtick. He continued to explain. "The actors add their bit. That is a composite effort. That's moviemaking, my dear. The audience goes home with a piece of your story in their pocket, forever." He was having the best time.

But Solley cautioned her, sounding wary, "When success happens right out of the gate, Summer, my dear one, from the get-go, it can be like a drug. Handling success is something a lot of people can't—don't— handle. I have faith in you. Your father turned out one hell of a strong lady. The woman pirate in your story has a semi-autobiographical bent. Tell me, does it?"

"If it makes you happy to think that, go ahead," Summer replied. It was part of their routine, for him to wrangle one small shred of personal history. Summer only smiled sweetly and said nothing. Now he had met his match. She was not an open book; her dad had taught her poker, and she played it well.

Summer said, "I'm sure you would have liked each other." She pictured them talking over her trials and tribulations.

Seeing there was no avenue to pursue this, Solley cleared his throat and tried to change the subject. "We'll need a score that will keep playing like the Energizer Bunny, one that becomes classic. Someone like Danny Elfman has that quality."

"Unbelievable," Summer said, shaking her head. "What about getting anyone to read something from an unknown writer?"

"Sometimes an unknown is just what's needed. New blood has new ideas. Everyone is looking to win the lottery. A fresh new writer with an amazing work. I think I know who to spring this on."

"You do? Tell me your plan." Summer was all ears.

"I've been known to cut a deal in seven figures for unknowns, Missy. Just leave this to me. I don't go anywhere without a plan."

"I have faith in you, Mr. Lester."

"I'm calling in some markers," he told her, rubbing his hands together. "I know we could have a hit on our hands. I have itchy palms—always an indication I'm right." He gave Summer a mock frown. "Lotus Productions has been optioning properties. Roger Medvey can pretty much write his own ticket, he has some kind of an overall with JVC and Sony. He's one of the few producers who will take a meeting on a property with breakthrough ideas. Yes, even from a novice."

Summer listened, enthralled. His positive attitude was catching.

"We have a history, Roger and me,' he said with a self-satisfied look, as if he'd hit on the solution to a difficult problem.

Summer was getting used to what appeared to be the flights in his head where he went from time to time to hatch these plans. They were like heat-seeking missiles. She knew he was plotting from the way he furrowed his heavily lined brow.

He said, "I'll see Roger this weekend."

"Where?" Summer felt cornered.

"He's docked in the marina, boobie." Looking rather pleased, he informed her, "Roger's having a cocktail party on his boat. Invited are some giants of moviemaking."

Summer only knew what she had read about Roger Medvey in all the trade publications. They cast him as a man with renegade attitudes, and his disdain for the Hollywood scene was no secret. He lived in Santa Fe, New Mexico, but he enjoyed a position in Hollywood others would kill for.

Founder and president of Lotus Production Company, he had mega hits to his credit and few bombs. Often seen on his arm in photographs was stunning successful Santa Fe sculptress Carole Titian, always described as his dear friend. Summer wondered exactly what that meant.

Knowing the sun was shining outside this dingy office, while others were enjoying it, drove Summer wild. They'd been working in the office since early morning and now it was past high noon. She was restless and hungry. The office smelled heavily of Solley's old cigars resting in the ashtray.

She told herself to be careful, or Solley would sense her mood and make her work late. She was also distracted now by the news he was going to be on the yacht while she worked the party. As if talking to himself, he offered, "This guy's a mensch."

"Who?" Summer inquired.

"Roger Medvey. He owns ninety percent of the stock in Lotus Productions." Solley went on and on. "Runs his empire by cell phone, fax, and FedEx. Roger lives outside of Hollywood, or on his yacht. Not a lot about him gets into print about his private life. He was always a loner. Not too many people really know him." Solley praised him again. "He's a solid mensch."

Standing and stretching, her arms above her head, she worked the kinks out of her sore neck and back from sitting tense for hours. Summer yawned, hoping Solley would take the hint.

The octogenarian could survive on endless cups of coffee and nervous energy. He made no move to quit for the day. "One could say I was somewhat instrumental in his coming to Hollywood," Solley admitted, rambling on. "His father wanted him in the family banking business. Roger went to USC film school, where he excelled. He was determined, not unlike you, my dear. He had a tremendous drive to succeed. He joined the ranks of the Hollywood wunderkinds before he was thirty."

Listening to Solley reminiscing about Roger Medvey, Summer could almost visualize his somewhat-Roman nose and his always- tanned face.

She'd seen many photos of him. Astride a horse, on his ranch. In publicity photos he commanded attention, whether dressed in cowboy boots, jeans, or tux.

Summer was incredulous at the suggestion. "Don't tell me you're going to pitch Roger Medvey!"

"Why not, Sum? Who else in this town has the personal and financial clout to do a project simply because he likes it?" Solley slid his hand back and forth over his shiny bald head, as if it were helping him think. "Your story is great. I like to cast the principals in my head. Who could do justice to the heroine? Someone very strong, and very beautiful. Let's see, who . . .?"

"The Irish rebel. Maybe an unknown should play the role of the pirate Patrick." Solley laughed out loud. The joke eluded Summer.

Sensing her restlessness, he said, "Okay, let's call it a day."

With a sigh of relief, Summer bolted out of the office with a quick goodbye and wave of her hand.

Chapter Seven

After a good night's rest and a respite from Solley, Saturday arrived bright and sunny. The afternoon before the Medvey affair, she spent the better part of the day resting in a lounge chair, soaking up sun she needed like a starving person needed bread. She drifted into a half doze, thought about the Academy Awards last year. She had worked the Governors Ball. It was her first opportunity to see the A-list of Hollywood royalty firsthand. Pretty heady stuff for a girl brought up on dreams of celluloid in the outback desert!

Solley Lester had held court at his special table that night. Nicolas Cage and Meryl Streep were his dinner partners. It was the first time Solley had observed Summer outside of his class.

She remembered how he gave her a warm smile of welcome, a peck on her cheek, and introduced her to the luminaries at his table. "Meet my student at the Institute who will be writing for you, no doubt."

Summer blushed at the wild compliment and escaped to the bar. Her excitement at being a part of the

Hollywood scene was eleven out of ten. It made her feel like she could levitate, though she was only then serving or tending bar.

That evening, dozens of celebrities came by Solley Lester's table, as if to pay homage to him. If Bernie Weldon, his driver of forty years, would allow it, Solley Lester would have been the party animal he'd once been. At eighty-five, he still enjoyed the glitz and glitter of show business. Summer saw as he became young again in the heady atmosphere of Tinseltown. He shed thirty years as he regaled the younger folk with stories considered legend.

Summer played back the events of that special night in her head, her eyes closed against the warmth of the sun. Her body felt relaxed for the first time in weeks. Could this be a dream realized? Would she be let in to that rarified air of the film industry?

* * *

After that awards dinner, she'd been invited to the after-party at Loren's Century City hi-rise condo as part of a small, select group of Loren's friends. They had relaxed while comparing notes, sharing champagne, and reliving the highlights of the special evening.

"Did you dig the gravity-defying Armani gowns the older stars wore?" Rehashing the evening, catty as she could be, Loren said, "How 'bout those ridiculous Zegna tuxes the Macho Stud Division came out in?

Puleeze. I thought Nehru was passé. Steven Seagal and Sylvester Stallone led the pack."

Loren babbled on about who was sleeping with who. Her hands were talking just as fast as her lips. Summer thought she was enormously entertaining as she went on aimlessly about who was out, and who should come out. Summer had been too tired to be charming. She just took it all in till her eyes would not focus.

"They'll be ripping the envelope with your name someday. I know it," Loren said. "Think, girl—a seat in the first few rows with all the other perspiring nominees. That's cool."

Imagining was a pastime Summer did now more often than not. With rejection and acceptance coming her way day by day like ping-pong balls.

Summer lathered on a lot of sheer suntan oil. Feeling as if she had deserted the world, she immersed herself in the stack of *Daily Varieties* and *Hollywood Reporters* Jerry had rounded up for her a few days ago. It was like a test a pilot faces, in the heat of the chase and the thrill of the hunt. Danger everywhere. This was her safari, the maze she needed to get through.

There was an article about Roger Medvey, dated four weeks ago, which she found interesting. Little was written about him personally; it might have been reverse public relations, no doubt. The news dealt more with his business opportunities. A peculiar sensation of warmth spread over her at the thought she would be meeting him.

Imagine how different it could be if she met him in his world, already famous for an award-nominated screenplay. Well, she wasn't, and it wasn't, so for now she would be tending his bar.

Few tenants at the house ever used the small patio or came out to the backyard. Spring flowers bloomed in the rich groomed soil and spring bulbs were starting to come up in the narrow beds. A little patch of paradise, lush and green, that afforded her a rare restive pastime. She daydreamed, glad to be alone.

No longer the green kid from the desert, she knew how formidable the competition could be. Solley seemed so sure she was going to sell her work. Summer felt assured he would be right.

With almost complete privacy on the patio, Summer undid her top and slid out of her bikini bottom to feel the warmth of the sun caressing her nude body, and she soon drifted off.

It wasn't until Jerry Simon appeared out of nowhere. In his best Jerry Lewis imitation, he screamed, "Lady!"

"Okay, so you caught me." Summer struggled to put the towel she was sitting on over her unclothed body.

"Pussycat, it's wasted on me." Jerry chuckled. "Babycakes, remember you said to let you know when it was witching time?" He tapped his wrist. "Four o'clock."

* * *

From the moment Summer stepped onto the Lazzara, she felt the pull of Roger Medvey's personality. As a man who had been described as having infinite good taste in all things, his yacht lived up to his press.

LA was Mecca for luxurious yachts. She had worked on a few. This seventy-six-foot-long Lazzara was a gorgeous boat.

There was fine, highly polished teak paneling on all the walls and custom wool carpeting three inches thick in a rich cream color covering the salon floor. Above a huge dining table that seated twelve was a six-foot round crystal chandelier fastened to a mirrored ceiling, shedding diamond sparkles over the table and setting a gracious mood.

Summer walked around the salon running her hand over the overstuffed couches covered in the softest embossed leather. An assortment of large colorful pillows made from American Indian weavings adorned them.

It was inviting. Summer found there was no disappointment here. None of the hostility toward comfort was apparent. She was aware this was pure, understated elegance she was admiring. She was curious to see the rest of the yacht, but resisted going below decks. She didn't know the cost of yachts, but was sure this one was worth many millions of dollars.

She perused Roger's book collection. Bookshelves were overflowing with books and magazines tucked into any niche wherever space allowed. With time to spare before guests arrived, she walked the upper deck, appreciating the beautiful balmy night. It was that perfect Southern California night the LA Chamber of Commerce liked to talk about. The soft sea breezes and balmy air, and the twinkling stars starting to make a light show, added to the glamour.

Back in the salon, Summer strolled by the beautifully arranged dinner buffet and admired the gorgeous spread of exotic foods. The caterers had laid out a luscious array of spicy Indonesian peanut chicken satay, pricey caviar in puff-pastry stars, shrimp with tortellini on bamboo skewers, and other assorted delicacies fit for the kings and queens of the film industry.

Since tending bar, Summer had become accustomed to trying the best of everything in foods still unusual to her palate. She still had a yen for a good taco, but her taste buds had definitely been educated.

Summer stepped behind the handsome bar. The bar top was made of hammered copper and gleamed with a bright patina. She arranged crystal glasses on it in various sizes, all engraved with the initials R.M., setting them on the back bar behind her. She couldn't resist pinging the crystal with her nails to hear the expensive sound. She wondered who of the illustrious tonight would sample the expensive champagnes chilling in the refrigerator: Dom Perignon, and the Medvey private-label wines.

She spotted Roger Medvey as he was coming up the beautiful Lucite staircase, looking very handsome. She could not stop staring at him. Descriptions of him in print, fresh in her mind, calling him "brilliant and complicated," only added to his allure. His pictures in magazines hadn't registered the magnetism of the man.

He was dressed in a lightweight gabardine business suit made of a beige fabric with a small pattern. His button-down collared shirt, unbuttoned two buttons down, made him look as if he were ready to relax after a hard day at the office. Summer wondered if that was a practiced pose.

Walking around the spacious cabin, he corrected the tilt of a lampshade, plumped a pillow, generally checking things out. No detail seemed too small for his attention. Exchanging a few words with one of the servers, they laughed at something. There was a relaxed feeling. It appeared to her he was no snob. As he walked toward the bar, he smiled at her. Answering his friendly smile, Summer smiled back. He planted himself on one of the barstools.

"What may I get for you?" she asked. She didn't address him by name.

"Perrier, twist of lemon. Please," he added.

She felt him assessing her with his eyes, as he might a valued acquisition, not missing a detail. It made her uncomfortable.

He looked more closely at the fresh, natural-looking girl, her freshly washed hair framing her face in soft waves. It was a beautiful face that glowed with good health and the blush of a tan, and the fresh scent of lavender. He took in every detail of the girl as she worked effortlessly.

The entire waitstaff, men and women, wore white streamlined cotton shirts with a black bow tie and smartly tailored black trousers. Such an outfit might make other girls look less than feminine, he thought, but on her it only enhanced her appeal.

Summer set his drink on the bar. Roger Medvey said, "Thank you," and gave her a warm smile as he took the glass and napkin. He started to leave, then, changing his mind, sat back down.

"Are you an actress . . .?" Reading her name tag, he called her by name. "Summer?"

"No, I'm a writer." She gave him a genuine smile, sure to add, "Who tends bar."

"Written anything?"

"I have a screenplay completed, but as the saying goes, I haven't quit my day job." She gave him another winsome smile.

"I'm always looking for new material," he said. Summer acknowledged this with a casual nod.

He was struck by her blinding good looks. There was none of the haughtiness of the female stars he knew, nor of the climbers who pursued him. Roger ran his hand through his sun-streaked hair. This girl seemed unimpressed by who he was.

"Summer . . . and your last name is?"

"Murphy. And I hope you will know my name when I try to get you to take a meeting with me."

"That seems like a perfect name for you." He nodded his approval. "Summer Murphy, nice. I'll remember you said that, when I'm trying to get past your secretary and she says, Summer who?"

Roger Medvey had a thing for soft, mellow women's voices. Hers was resonant and sexy.

"You knew who I was all along, admit it," he said in an unassuming voice.

"I have seen your pictures. Who in Hollywood hasn't?" Summer nevertheless gave him a coy look. "Host of the vessel."

He gave her a winning smile. "I'd like to find out more about your writing." Reluctantly he stood up. "Be back for refills." Giving her a winning smile, he went off to greet his guests. Roger Medvey thought the girl was a beauty. He would make it a point to ask Mel or Steve Carey for her number and a brief bio.

Summer had noticed his square, strong, manicured hands that were very callused. Useful hands, she thought. Several times during the evening, she caught him glancing her way. Each time she felt a strong pang of excitement that was totally confusing to her.

Solley Lester came aboard after most of the guests

had arrived. He was with Jeffrey Katzenberg. From Summer's vantage point she watched as they walked around the salon greeting people. Jeffery Katzenberg had lectured once at the Institute. He was a short, bearded, wiry individual who looked as if he were moving even when he was standing still. Summer got a charge out of observing Solley with all these high rollers. He was in his element, and he looked right at home among them.

He'd often told Summer he really didn't like cocktail parties. Numerous times she'd heard him say, "It is a necessary evil. The party circuit lets everyone take each other's temperature, all a part of the tap dance called deal-making. Remember that." Solley liked to call himself "The Broker-Meister."

He did a theatrical double take when he approached the bar, pretending to be surprised to see her. He took an unlit cigar from his mouth.

"Here you are, Miss Murphy, as bewitching as ever."

"Don't be buttering me up," Summer said in the most lilting Irish brogue. "And there are no ashtrays anywhere on board. It's true; Roger Medvey runs a tight ship, Solley." Summer continued to lecture him. "The designated smoking room seems to be just outside on the helm cockpit. This isn't the Friars Club, Mr. Lester."

He dabbed the cigar out, pouting. Summer was sure was not on the level.

"Your being here sort of cramps my style tonight," Solley said.

She shrugged. "How so?"

He looked around the boat, at the people splintered off into tight little groups, deep in conversation. "Look around. These are some of the most powerful people in film and television here tonight. I'm here to talk to them about your script. You see, I want Roger to hear about it from others. That way you remain a mystery. He won't have any idea if the wunderkind is a dish or not."

"A dish. That's an expression from the forties?" she asked. She was incredulous. "I'm just one of the hired help."

"Medvey is quite a catch, don't you think, Miss Murphy?"

"I don't know him, so I can't say. He's been voted bachelor of the year for two years running. From what I've read, he doesn't look unhappy. Besides, you're selling my screenplay, not me on Roger." She mugged a satisfied smile.

"You're one exquisite package, Miss Murphy." Solley's thoughts were telegraphed across his expressive face. "I never go to a meeting without a strategy, pussycat. I'm dealing with heavy hitters. Your rewrite is good. They'll be talking the deal I want, or I'll be out among 'em till I bring home the bacon!"

"That simple, huh?" Summer's eyes darted around the crowded room looking for Roger. He was nowhere in sight. She had the oddest feeling of loss at losing sight of him.

A man wearing a loud silk-print Nicole Miller shirt and a heavy Israeli accent asked Summer for a white wine spritzer. Almost every other guest had on a coat and tie. He settled onto the barstool with a big sigh, then pretended as if he just now recognized Solley Lester. He thrust his fleshy hand at him. "Moshe Diamond, we met at the Friars in New York last year before the nominations came out for the Academy Awards. Solley, how are ya?"

Solley took the obligatory handshake, though his face looked vacant of recognition.

Summer delivered the spritzer to the countertop. He scooped it up and he took a noisy swig.

"Nice ta see you. You have maybe a new property? I'm buyink if your sellink," Moshe offered.

Searching his memory for a millisecond, Solley made slits of his eyes trying to recall the face in front of him. He took a stab. "Zodiac Productions, the kung fu feature!" Solley raised his chin in recognition and snapped his fingers, trying to remember the name. *The Journey*. Right? Was a great formula picture with lots of special effects."

"Formula, what . . . are kidding me?" Moshe defended his picture's worth. "It was a bullet at the box office, first three weeks broke fifty million."

Solley said evenly, "Yeah, for a story with no plot,

not bad." He smoothed the lapel of his expensive suit, which had Savile Row written all over it.

"By you, it's not bad?" Moshe got up to leave the bar, noticeably upset. He picked up his drink like so many marbles and went in search of greener pastures. The colorful shirt was visibly talking to himself.

Solley wet the end of his expensive, illegal, Cuban cigar, still unlit, and said, "You see that guy, Summer?" He gestured with his stogie. "His feature, *The Journey*, was a piece of crap! Jeez!" His eyes swept over the room. "There's nothing more desirable than something someone else wants."

Out of the corner of his eye, Solley noticed Roger glancing in Summer's direction—again in the past few minutes. Little got by him. "I take it you and Roger have already been introduced."

"I served him earlier. We chitchatted." Summer smiled at Solley's reaction.

"I plan to tell Roger that Spielberg is thinking of optioning a terrific new writer. I'll talk to everyone but Roger tonight, so when I do call him he will be interested. I've got to circulate your name, get some publicist to dream up a background story. He will be interested, trust me. You can take that to the bank. Curiosity, it works all the time. Look around this floating palace, boobie, deals cut tonight by these powerhouses will affect careers for long years to come. Maybe in the bargain a few Academy Awards are listing off the bow."

Solley slid off the high barstool, jamming his cigar back into his mouth, and walked into the crowded room toward the buffet table. He sampled some hors d'oeuvres, then walked jauntily into the fray. He could have been a small knight jousting with the big boys. The rest of the evening went without incident. It was a peculiar gig, with Solley on board. Roger made several turns at the bar. This gave Summer a rush, though she was determined to stay cool.

Chapter Eight

At two thirty in the morning, there was little more than the glittering lights from boats in their docks. The yacht was framed in an opaque, velvety black sky with few stars remaining. The fog lay like a gray blanket over Marina Del Rey in the early morning hours. Steve Carey descended the steps from the ship to the dock and offered his hand to Summer. He had insisted on taking her home. They hadn't seen each other in a long time and the drive would give them a chance to catch up. As they entered the freeway Steve filled her in on the past few months.

"Eventmakers will do Roger Medvey's charity ball in Santa Fe next month. I want you to come along with the team. It will take three days to set up a beautiful evening in historic old Santa Fe. I'd like you to go as event coordinator. We need a really hot babe in our crew. The money's really good." Steve stressed the financial perks.

"Never been to Santa Fe," Summer said. "It sounds like a little bit of heaven. Maybe?"

Steve Carey was a hell of a catch: a handsome Ivy

League guy, clean-cut good looks, a successful businessman. He was enamored with Summer, had been ever since the day she interviewed for the job, and she was aware of it. But there was no spark. Not like the bolt of adrenaline she felt after meeting Roger Medvey.

"Summer, we're talking three days, a long weekend. Mel got Hootie and the Blowfish to entertain for the Indian School. Roger Medvey liked that and gave us this charity. It's like a whole new market for us. Don't say no, Sum." Every chance he got, Steve Carey let her know how much he liked her.

They took the freeway. There was hardly a car on the road at that hour.

Steve parked in front of her house with the motor still running. Summer could read between the lines of his request.

Finally she said, "How can I refuse such a deal? Count me in."

With a quick brush of her lips on his cheek, she started to exit the car, her hand on the door handle. Steve shut the motor off and moved to exit but Summer said, "Don't get out the driver's side. On Western Avenue it could be dangerous, only one lane left is open. I'm all right, thanks for the ride. Send me the info about Santa Fe." And she walked briskly to the house.

Steve watched her leave with his lights on till she closed the door. He realized she didn't feel the same about him. It was a real downer, but maybe that would change. He thought he was in love with her.

* * *

The rewrites of *The Pirate and the Lady* had gone faster than a California forest fire fanned by the devilish Santa Ana winds. Over the next few weeks, Summer worked like a crazed person. She wanted to work the event in Santa Fe. It would take tending bar for months to make the kind of money they were paying her.

She wondered if Roger would remember her should they meet. She searched the newspapers for any scrap of news about him. Lilly Crystal, who was starring in Lotus Production's feature *Manhattan*, was his date for the New York premiere. The photo op made them look very cozy together. Summer experienced vexation whenever she saw that picture—the actress held on to Roger as if he were her possession.

She took a marked dislike to Ms. Crystal on principle alone, that she was famous. Summer almost wished there were just Carole Titian to worry about. The list had to be longer than two.

The script satisfied Solley in record time. Summer would not be hidden behind a bar—she would be mingling with the honored guests at Roger's Santa Fe charity affair.

* * *

SANTA FE, NEW MEXICO

The many Indians who sat outside the town square selling their wares were there again, just as Summer had seen them the day before. She drove past them on her way out to the hardware store in DeVargas Shopping Center. She traveled in a rented Jeep on the Old Santa Fe Trail to Paseo de Peralta Road, carefully following a map, to get some last-minute items to decorate the main ballroom. It was a picture-perfect Southwestern day. Peonies were in bloom in profusion all over Santa Fe. The blossoms lent a heady scent to the crisp, seven-thousand-foot altitude. The late-afternoon sky had a clarity and brilliance Summer had never seen anywhere.

Every view was a painting. If this was Wonderland, then she felt like Alice. Perhaps that was the secret to all the artists who migrated there from all over the world. The sky had a light that was luminous, enchanting, with a myriad of color splashed across the firmament. To think she had almost decided to skip this treat. Bless Solley for his pressure and prodding and torment, and bless Steve Carey for insisting she come.

After just one day in Santa Fe, Summer knew it was never going to be enough time to explore. There was so much she wanted to see and experience. The meshing of three cultures, Native American, pioneer, and Hispanic, made the town so exciting.

Yesterday, Roger Medvey was nowhere to be seen

while she was in and out of Quail Run attending to the details of the formal affair. What if he had merely lent his name to the charity, never intending to make an appearance the way many celebrities did?

Summer found the hardware store and dove into a parking space. The clerk was helpful and she found everything in record time. Preparing to leave, having paid for her purchases, Summer looked toward the door and saw Roger Medvey coming in with another man. Juggling several parcels in her hands, and a little flustered at the sight of him, she dropped a bag of nails. They spread over the red clay tiles like so many ants in search of a hill. Summer struggled to hold on to her other packages without losing any more of them.

Coloring slightly from embarrassment, Summer dropped down to her knees to retrieve the mess. Roger walked off into the aisles of the store, obviously looking for something. A man with a map of Ireland on his cherubic face bent down to help her. The good Samaritan wore a cap of glen plaid. Tufts of wiry white hair overflowed his cap. He sported a smart, clipped, white Van Dyke beard.

When he had picked everything up, he tipped his cap. "Here you are, lass," he said as he handed her the nails. "I'm Danny O'Hara, but you call me O'Hara, as all my friends do."

Summer felt the heat rising high on her cheeks, her heart pounding in her chest. "I was afraid I'd be here all day. I really have to get back, thank you. It was kind of you." She dusted off her pants and clutched the parcels closer to her heart. "I can't thank you enough."

"It was my pleasure, young lady," he answered, looking the girl over.

Roger Medvey strode over to join them at the counter. He wore leather boots, jeans, and a plaid flannel shirt, looking like a fabulous Ralph Lauren ad. His clothes were smeared with what looked like paint. There was a slight dew of perspiration at his hairline. He still looked like the best thing since chopped liver— a Solley Lester expression Summer loved to use.

A feigned look of enlightened recognition covered his face. Roger teased, "Ah, the pretty bartender on the yacht. You serve up a perfect Perrier and lemon, Summer Murphy!"

Summer smiled at his attempt at comedy. She was thrilled he remembered her name.

"Be actin' neighborly, Mr. M. Tell me, who might this delightful Colleen be?" the Irishman coaxed.

"I never forget a sexy bartender." Roger bit his lower lip and angled his head off to the side as he sized her up in her jeans and T-shirt. His grin gave her the seal of approval.

"You're gorgeous and I make it a habit to remember pretty women." He pronounced it the way her dad had, *garr-geous*, as the Irish pronounced it. "This is Miss Murphy, a writer, Mr. O'Hara."

"Mr. Medvey's having—"

Roger interrupted, "Danny O'Hara is my major-domo. He's a jack of all trades, keeps my life in order."

Roger clapped a hand on Danny's shoulder, making it clear there was great camaraderie between the two men. "She's a Solley Lester client. You remember I alluded to the language in her script. Very salty! I was telling you about the screenplay I just read, yes?" He prodded O'Hara for a response, who agreed all too readily and adopted a posture of interest.

Summer wondered if their little tap dance was totally kosher. Laying an adorable smile on the two of them, she said, "Thanks for the compliment."

"Solley tells me you're already working on the sequel." Giving her his full attention, he said, "Sequels can be potential money cows these days, and great if the screenplay is any good. Will your sequel be as good as your first venture?"

Uncomfortable that Solley Lester had hatched a gross exaggeration at her expense, Summer fought to maintain her composure. She'd done all she could to finish the first script. She made a move to leave, gathering up her packages, when Roger stopped her.

"Wait. I'm having a small cocktail party at my home tonight, before the gala tomorrow," he said. "Can you come? I'd like to see if your language skills transcend the written page, Miss Murphy." He conveyed a naughty wickedness in his inquiry, and she knew he referred to the racy language in her script. Summer melted under his wide, accepting smile.

"Please say you'll come. I live just inside Wilderness Gate," he insisted.

Summer looked at her watch, calculated the rest of the afternoon's work in her head. "I've really got to get these things back. I would like to see at least one house in Santa Fe. They're all hidden behind adobe walls or coyote fences," she acquiesced. "What time?"

Roger seemed relieved she had accepted. "It will be just a few good friends at six thirty. Mr. O'Hara can pick you up. Where are you staying?"

"I am at the St. Francis," she said to Danny, giving him a smile that made him melt.

"I'll be out in front waiting for you at six fifteen," O'Hara assured her.

"Come on." Roger took O'Hara's arm. "Let's not keep Miss Murphy a minute more." He called to the clerk on his way out with a wave of his hand.

"Put three toggle bolts on my bill, Cecile." The cashier didn't look up, just gave him a wave indicating it was done. "Bye, Mr. M., Mr. O," she called after them.

Summer went through the afternoon replaying the encounter in the hardware store. She felt a rush of heat in her body and wondered, *Was that infatuation?* Each time she found another tidbit to think on. Remembering Roger's eyes, so dark and intense, so blue. It sent shivers through her just thinking about him. He was one of the most attractive men she had ever met.

In the hotel gift shop, Summer had admired a brightly colored paisley shawl earlier in the day, but felt she couldn't afford it. At the end of the day, she bought the shawl, putting it on her credit card. She left herself barely enough time to shower, do her hair, apply makeup, and dress.

Loren Palmer had loaned her a Donna Karan black strapless silk taffeta cocktail dress to take on this trip for some unexpected occasion. It clung to her, accentuating her perfectly beautiful, athletic body. Summer smiled at her image in the full-length mirror. Roger Medvey invaded her thoughts, and that doused her like a hot wave. She felt her cheeks ablaze.

She wanted to look her best this evening—for him. Also borrowed from Loren was a Judith Leiber evening purse that she carried in the palm of her hand. The silly thing couldn't hold much more than some money and lipstick. It was a tiny, glittery thing that resembled a turtle. Loren confided it had cost over three thousand dollars. That made Summer feel giddy—it cost more than her entire earnings for that year.

She grabbed the phone from the nightstand when its ringing interrupted her musings.

"Hello," she answered, still in a fog over Roger Medvey.

A frenetic Mel Carey spoke in his usual staccato and

went on about the continuity of details. He wanted everyone assembled an hour earlier than planned. Before she could say anything, he hung up.

Summer sighed and sat down on the bed, dejected, fingering the expensive shawl she'd hawked her soul for. Splurging went against her grain. She'd better cancel. She took the phone book out of the nightstand to look up Roger Medvey's number, but there was no listing. Summer gave a sigh of relief. She really wanted to size up Carole Titian. Maybe this was for the best. She argued with herself about going, and then said out loud to the sturdy Southwestern furniture in the room, "The hell with it. I'm going!"

Catching sight of the clock, Summer took one last glimpse of her reflection, felt satisfied, and sailed all the way down the carpeted stairs of the Hotel St. Francis. It was called the wedding hotel because of the double-wide staircase built in the 1800s for the nuptials of the daughter of the man who owned it.

* * *

O'Hara was waiting curbside when Summer came out, just as he promised. He gave her the friendliest smile as he helped her into the Jeep like a fragile package. Summer couldn't remember being so fawned over.

The Irishman pointed out the landscape and historical sights up Canyon Road as they drove into the hills, out of the town square. He casually mentioned small gatherings were Roger's preference when entertaining at home: "There'll be just a few neighbors coming to-night—those with the price of a thousand dollars a plate for the fundraiser." He added, "Miss Titian flew in for the gala. She is, after all, a dear friend."

O'Hara continued to point out how hard it was to tell the difference in the ages of adobes built in the 1700s nestled in with newer adobes on the canyon roads. Those adobe walls and coyote fences hid the houses and gardens entirely from sight.

"When the sun dips behind the Sangre de Cristo mountain range, 'twill be a flaming red ball. Roger's twenty acres were handpicked by the angels. He placed the house in the perfect place for such sunsets."

Summer loved the Irishman's brogue.

All of a sudden, pinyon trees surrounded them on the dirt roads they passed into Wilderness Gate. They were against the national forest. Summer felt closer to the sky here wrapped in a sensual and textural environment.

That spring evening was of such beauty, Summer was sure she'd always remember it: The clarity of the sky with hues of blue and violets and soft yellows. Wispy white clouds like miles of tulle, resembling the trains of bridal gowns. The sun low in the sky, the promised globe of bright red. The light had changed drastically to a soft amber and smoky purple in the twelve minutes it took to get there.

Like the rest of Santa Fe, Roger's house was a surprise since it was totally enclosed behind high adobe walls. On the highest hill of the property, the house emerged out of the land from the red clay soil.

The large two-story entry hall was all opposing curves with shiny plaster walls scented of beeswax. The iron gates were intricately rounded and sensuously detailed, as were the hand railings. The furnishings ran the gamut from western contemporary to oriental art. Pieces were cleverly put together in a relaxed way. The architecture was more beautiful than any house she'd ever seen in magazines. His house was surprisingly cozy for such a large, imposing home.

Walking quickly through the house, O'Hara led Summer to where voices could be heard. She glanced at the art on the walls, and no surprise, there was sculpture or two by his dear friend, Carole Titian. Summer wished she didn't like the pieces, but she thought they were wonderful.

Danny guided her into the great room. Roger saw them arrive and left the man he was talking to. He moved to greet her. "Just the guest I was looking for." He smiled wide. "Let me take your wrap."

"No, thank you." Summer draped her shawl tightly over her arms. "I tried to call you to cancel, but your phone's not listed. I can only stay a few minutes. I have to be at the ballroom earlier than expected."

"You look great, I'm glad you came. Come with me,

I want you to meet my friends." He walked her around the room, handing her a flute of champagne from a silver tray that was being passed around, while he made perfunctory introductions.

Having done the polite thing, he walked Summer toward open terrace doors. He wrapped his arm around her waist and they walked out together to see the sun going down in a blaze. He plucked a tiny rose from a terra cotta planter and handed it to her.

She sniffed its fragrance. "Delicious," she admitted.

He turned her around and stood behind her, facing the setting sun. "I want you to have the best view. Over the last month, I've wondered what you were doing, where you were." His voice sounded sincere. "I don't like to mix business with pleasure, but rules are meant to be broken. Your screenplay is . . . wonderful. And you were hard to forget."

"With all the women you meet?" Summer shook her head, showing mock disappointment.

"I don't have to pitch you. Why don't you believe me?"

She was suspicious of Roger's overabundance of charm. After all, he was a major player. He'd been voted bachelor of the year twice—so the rags said.

"When Carole's away, Roger plays, eh?" She just smiled and shook her head. She turned to face him, her green eyes raising to his of deep blue. With a peevishness she meant, she asked, "What about your dear friend Carole?"

"Carole?"

Their eyes were locked for a quick moment. She said it again. "Yes. You know, your dear friend."

"Her mare's ready to foal tonight. She called an hour ago to beg off. Carole lives on the next spread." He tossed that off as casually as if he were talking about a pen pal.

Summer thought, Carole Titian had been at his side for the longest time . . . for years. It had to be more serious between them than he implied. Well, he was as crafty as a sidestepping matador. She was sure he was throwing the bull. Roger Medvey was apparently proving to be like most of the scoundrels in Hollywood.

"Do you think O'Hara could take me? I really need to go." Summer redressed her shawl tightly around her shoulders.

"Yes, of course."

He led Summer by the hand to where O'Hara was chatting with a group of people. Roger excused himself and asked O'Hara to drive Summer to the event.

She was deep in thought trying to figure out what had gone on out there on the terrace. Why had Roger acted as if Carole Titian was to be taken for granted? She replayed the conversation in her head. Thanks to Carole Titian needing to help birth a horse, Summer had Roger all to herself. A wicked smile crept across her face. Two could play at this game. Summer told herself it was his position of power in motion pictures that made him so irresistible. She intended to pursue the friendship, for all that he could help her career.

She smiled at Danny O'Hara, trying to be good company. "Sorry, Danny, I'm caught up in the details of the gala."

"Roger seems really taken with you." O'Hara swung his eyes over Summer to punctuate his remark. He wanted to see her reaction, but he was busy keeping his eyes on the road.

"You have to be kidding. Mr. Bachelor of the Year? I don't think so."

He smiled like a diffident devil with a secret. Wise Danny O'Hara could see a woman's face and know what she was thinking.

Another ten-minute ride and they were at the beautiful Quail Run Country Club. Elegantly dressed in formal Southwestern wear, the guests wore designer suede gowns, studded in all kinds of jewels. They came decked out in exquisite and rare Indian turquoise jewelry. Diamond-studded accessories sparkled on both men and women. They wore boots in designs and colors fashioned from exotic hides. This was signature fashion for these people, patrons of major charities in Santa Fe. The price of dinner here was a mere $1,000 a plate.

The Carey brothers had not let any detail go unattended. The guests were getting their money's worth. They would go home with a swag bag full of goodies, just like the ones the Academy Awards did.

The magnificent ballroom was decorated in a mono-chromatic contemporary Southwestern motif. Huge, five-tier wrought-iron chandeliers with magnificent crystal pendants sparkled down on tables richly decorated with fine china, silver dinnerware, and crystal glasses. At the center of every table were several large amethyst geodes surrounded by peonies on the ivory linens.

Numerous times Summer traversed the room, checking the smallest of details to see everything went as planned. During the evening, she mingled and danced with a number of guests. When she did the tango with actor Gene Hackman, the other guests watched and applauded. Roger finally got around to asking her to dance late in the evening.

His arms around her made her feel warm and pro-tected; the level of desire she felt was surprising. They danced in silence. Summer felt comfortable in his arms, and she was in another world.

At the end of the dance Roger resisted letting her go, but duty called. She was, after all, the hostess for the evening. All year Summer had avoided any in-volvements, refusing any and all who approached her. Now, of all people, Roger Medvey was making noises like the typical Hollywood mogul, making a move on her as if she were free bread on a restaurant table. For the longest time, no one had affected her like this. She hoped he wouldn't turn out to be a shit.

Close to midnight, Roger stepped onto the stage

and took the mike to thank half a dozen large contributors to the charity. Unexpected was Carol Burnett delivering her Tarzan call, to the delight of the guests, when he presented the Indian School with a check for $1,200,000. Roger drew from the raffle tickets for a Mercedes SL400. The room hummed with anticipation when he called the numbers. The lucky winner stepped up to the stage to thunderous applause.

The evening had been a resounding success. Summer was elated and wished there was no end to it. Several times during the evening she'd caught Roger tracking her with his eyes, leaving her feeling wired. At the end of the evening when all the guests had gone, he drifted over to where she was working with the rental company, sorting out the bills.

"Can I interest you in a nightcap, Miss Murphy, when you're all done?"

"You know, what I really would like is a messy hamburger." She gave him a winsome smile. "I never got to eat that delicious dinner tonight. Too busy and a little nervous, at first. Do you think something's open this late?"

"Sure, I know a place," he said with a take-charge attitude. "We need to fly."

"Whoa, where is this place?" Summer laughed at the thought.

"Miss Murphy, trust me. You're on my turf now." He had a mischievous smile plastered from ear to ear.

"Sure. I trust you like a ganef."

"I see Solley Lester's teaching you his special brand of show-biz Yiddish. This is the hamburger from heaven," Roger assured her.

"How can a girl resist something from heaven? When I'm through counting china, I'll meet you in the bar." Summer got her second wind after being up for twenty hours.

Roger Medvey's power in Hollywood was enormously appealing. She must keep her distance, try to at least cool it a little, till Solley got the script slotted for production somehow.

Chapter Nine

Roger drove them to a small airfield on the outskirts of Santa Fe, where he settled Summer into a small one-engine plane. They took off and landed in Albuquerque in less than fifteen minutes. From the airport they took a cab to the Cantina Hamburgers stand. It was open all night out on the road leading to I-15. The cars lined up as if it were the middle of the afternoon. It was a popular place.

The lighting coming off the building lit up the desert. There were picnic tables out in front, where they sat munching on four-inch-high burgers.

"This is the best cheeseburger I've ever had," Summer said, too hungry to make polite conversation. It was literally the first thing she'd had to eat all day.

She stared at Roger. He looked like what she had been missing in her life. She had not kissed a man in six months. She had thought of nothing but her work and then submerging herself in it, to forget the sorrow of her father's death. She liked everything about

Roger, his looks, humor, position in Hollywood, but he was a puzzle, flirtatious and charming.

She finished the burger with relish. She hadn't had an appetite for life until she met Roger Medvey. She'd been sleepwalking through her days till now. Work was her constant companion.

When they touched back down in Santa Fe, the sun was starting to come up. Handing her down to the ground from the plane, Roger asked, "About that nightcap at my house tonight. It is typical Santa Fe." He looked as fresh as if the evening had just begun.

Summer laughed at the way this was going. "What night? Looks like morning to me." She felt sated from the whole experience of Santa Fe. The plane ride had capped it off.

"I have to leave tomorrow for LA, Roger. I've slept maybe three hours back to back for two days. If I do collapse, just see I make my plane tomorrow. Promise?" It was a qualified yes.

Roger stared at her like he wanted to burn her image into his memory. It was a look women know all too well.

Damn, Summer thought, *only a couple of hours and here I'm forgetting about my promise to play it cool, keep my distance. Where is this going?* She worried at the speed this was going.

Fool! She kept repeating in her head. *You fool.*

Chapter Ten

Sex

Without flipping any lights on, Summer and Roger made their way through the back halls of his house. He stopped just beside some open double doors and took Summer in his arms, turned up her face, and kissed her with such a ferociousness that in that moment, with heat and urgency, they struggled to remove each other's clothes in tacit agreement.

He tossed her evening bag, then her shawl. She clawed at his tux jacket, got it off, and threw it on the floor. Greedily he kissed her face, shoulders, and neck as he removed her shoulder straps, while smoothly unzipping her dress. Summer returned the frenzy of his kisses. Roger's hands moved roughly over the smooth skin of her bare back, jangling his nerves and making his breath become short. His mouth covered hers and he whispered something she could not hear or understand. She stepped out of the circle of her dress. He reached for her hand, leading her into his room and pulling her onto a turned-down bed.

Summer's blood ran hot.

Roger consumed the fragrance of her hair, kissing her ears, murmuring endearments, creating sensations she never dreamed she could feel.

Fleetingly she thought, *Too damn late to act coy.* She was hungry for his lips and hands, and only here and now counted. When he gave them to her she returned his passion with a crescendo of desire mounting moment by moment.

Lost in the pleasure of that desire, the exploration of their uncharted bodies, they lay with the silvery moon casting a beam of light across the bed from a large open window, silhouetting their bodies against the shiny waxed walls. Summer's breasts rose and fell, her body writhing and arching to his demanding touch, while shadows on the wall made erotic images of a rhythmic love dance. Love sounds emitted from their lips through the strangle of their breath. His mouth sought the taste of her breasts, and his throat ached from the waves of pleasure. Her moans fueled his need.

They wrapped limbs around limbs in exploration of their bodies, tangled into one hot and pulsating heartbeat. When Roger took her, making them one, they expressed their sensual gratification with spasms of pleasure. Summer gasped, his name choked in her throat. She embraced him with abandon.

The sheets rustled from their thrashing. He returned her message of want and desire by holding fast to her, greedy to feel and express that need.

They lay in the dark, used up, listening to each other's labored breath, the wonderment of these love moments unspoken. He caught her hair with his fingers and held the silken threads. There had been little tenderness in him moments before, only raw animal need. Now he touched her eyebrows, face, the tip of her nose. His tenderness surprised her. She had no idea she could open herself up to anyone this way. Perhaps it was because he was such a skillful lover.

They fell back against the soft, warm down pillows, holding each other spoon-fashion, and fell asleep in the moon-glow. The large glass window remained clouded from the heat of their passion.

* * *

When Summer awoke, for a few brief seconds she didn't know where she was. Roger came in fully dressed and bent down to nuzzle her neck.

"Summer, are you ready to get up and face the world?"

She sat up, clutching the sheet to her chest, and asked where her clothes were. She had a memory of the night before and it brought a blush to her cheeks.

"Wouldn't you like to have some breakfast?"

"What time is it?" She searched the room for a clock and found none.

"Two in the afternoon, sweetheart."

"Two! You've got to be kidding me, my plane . . . Oh my god!"

His laugh was uncontrollable. He looked like the cat who'd caught the canary.

"How could I wake you? You looked so beautiful lying there. You still look beautiful, sweetheart."

Humor danced in her eyes. "My plane ticket was nonrefundable. I'm not so rich." She suddenly saw the ridiculousness of the situation. " Marooned, how lucky can a girl get? I don't know whether to be angry that you let me sleep, or what. This is so not like me."

However, she didn't want to ruin what they'd had last night. "Is the train less money than the plane?" she asked, hopeful to make the switch.

"Wrong, sweetness, costs more. Besides, it takes thirteen hours to get to LA." He sat down next to her and nuzzled her neck. "Just the thought of you going anywhere makes me cringe, Summer. You know, it's not only two o'clock in the afternoon, love. It's Tuesday! Poor baby, all that fooling around." He smiled the smile of the bedeviled.

Sitting next to her, he absorbed her scent and it sent him into a tailspin.

"I already called Solley and he says not to worry. See, your agent has you covered."

He kissed her hungrily, but held her tenderly. When her breath caught in her throat, she joined her tongue with his. He slid his hand over her body in a soft and sensual motion. She felt like a stroked cat.

She called out his name, arching her body to meet his, as he tore off his clothes in a few swift movements and slipped beside her in the bed. The first time there had been uncontrolled sex; this time there was tenderness.

Afterward, they lay naked and spent. Sweat and sex permeated the room, dual scents of their passion intermingled. Summer opened her eyes to look at Roger, wanting to take in every detail of him.

"Don't go back to LA just yet," he whispered, kissing Summer behind her ear.

"Roger, I have my work. Solley's helping me sell my script. It's not possible for me to stay, especially now. I have a career."

"Do you think old Solley Lester's in cahoots with my parents?" Roger asked half in jest. "They think I've debauched enough. They'd like to bounce something on their knees before they get too weak to pick it up. Solley did talk me into reading your script, but I think he had an alternative method to his madness. So . . .?"

"Debauched, now there's a word. What do you mean he talked you into reading my script? You said you liked it. You told me when I met you in the store that you thought it was, well . . . interesting. When you mentioned it to Mr. O'Hara. What can I believe?"

Roger rhythmically caressed her hair. "It's no secret I've had my share of starlets. Bimbos are not exactly the sharpest knives in the drawer. You can't bring them home to Mama. That's why Carole Titian accompanies me whenever possible. It's all for the benefit of the press. It's just a convenience. I got fed up with all of the Hollywood tap dance a while back." He waved a hand to express what it all meant. "In Hollywood, it is hard to know real from not real."

"You're telling me you and Carole Titian have an arrangement?" Summer moved away from him. She felt dizzy with this information.

" Carole is not your lover? That's what you'd have me believe?"

"No, she's not, nor ever has been. Carole would rather stay home on her ranch with her horses and dogs and her girlfriend."

"Her girlfriend!" She exhaled a sigh of relief. It took her a long minute to grasp what he'd meant.

"Darling girl, Carole is devoted to her trainer, Anne Winslow, the best horse trainer in the Southwest. They've been a couple and have lived together for many years. She's still a very," and they said it together, "dear friend."

That sent them into belly laughs. His eyes were shining and his lips curved into a warm smile. He cupped her face. "I'm not going to let you out of my life now that I found you. I'll take you back to LA, but only if you promise to like Carole Titian. She really is my friend."

"I can be a semi-understanding woman when the circumstances are right." She smiled her most engaging smile. "Oh, no problem, no problem at all."

Summer had a will of iron. When she wanted something, nothing could stand in her way. She knew now in just forty-eight hours, she wanted Roger Medvey in the worst way. She also wanted all of the good things he could do for her career. "Tell me what you liked about *The Pirate and the Lady!*"

Summer tossed back the covers and left the bed naked. She walked regally to the bathroom without the slightest bit of self-consciousness, not waiting for his answer.

* * *

After her heady weekend in Santa Fe, Summer took stock of her roller-coaster feelings for Roger Medvey. Using his toothbrush, she brushed and spit out the cool minty toothpaste. She looked in the mirror and thought she looked prettier than usual. Her naturally curly hair formed a halo of blond around her flushed face.

Maybe like the song, she thought. It was too hot not to cool down.

It had been foolish and impulsive of her to jump into bed with one of the most powerful men in Hollywood. There was no going back. This was either the beginning or a bitter end. She was already in love with Roger. Or was it lust? She had her father's pragmatic logic, and she figured the affair had nowhere to go from Santa Fe. He had unlimited access to all of the pulchritude in Hollywood, New York, and Europe, so why her? Unless . . .

Chapter Eleven

Roger returned from Europe and didn't call Summer. Solley dropped the ball and she found out he had been in LA for more than a week. The cat was out of the bag. It caused her heart to ache. Summer felt that first stab of possessiveness. Roger might have put her on his to-do list, but it had taken more than a week after that for him to call her. When he did, she was obviously guarded and distant, and he detected the burn.

Not wanting to admit to herself or anyone else that he was essential to her well-being, Summer put up a brave front. His seeming indifference was pissing her off. When Roger took her to dinner at Spago's, he told her he would be out of town again for the next few weeks. He acted affectionate, but he seemed worried and preoccupied. Though he said he wished they could be together, she was beginning to wonder. What gives?

There was something bothering him, and he was guarded. She pleaded fatigue that night. He took her home early at her request. She wondered if she was being silly, making a mountain out of a molehill.

So much for their affair. Since Summer's sojourn in Santa Fe, in the following weeks she had gone out on a few dates, when Loren insisted. One had been with a well-known actor who was totally into himself, and one with a studio accountant who sucked Tic Tacs. Two gigantic bores.

Roger called her a few times that week while he was in London on business. He was chatty and asked how the script was going. They kept it light. She told him about Solley's hopes for the screenplay. He didn't offer any advice, only saying, "Take no prisoners, Summer. The Lips will squeeze the last drop of blood from a stone to get you the deal that's right."

The sound of his voice put her in a mild trance. He made the most interesting soft L-sound.

Suddenly she was tangled up in someone else's life. That was frightening to her. Summer defined her life as being independent, not another person's appendage. Loren thought maybe she was hiding something. She'd tried to caution Summer against Roger. They set up a lunch date at the Warner Bros. Studio commissary, just like old times, but what was bugging her friend?

She said, "Pussycat, Roger's got a reputation for quickie romances. Only Warren Beatty holds the greater heartbreak record. Now he's married to Annette Bening. How 'bout I fix you up with a musician I know that's hot on the charts, and has a long booking in LA?"

The waiter took their orders and brought two goblets of water with a basket of great bread.

"Musicians don't interest me—not the hard-rock crowd you hang out with, Loren," Summer teased. The waiter poured them more water, as if protecting them from a drought.

"Sum, you can't sit around and wait for this guy. Besides, he's GQ, geographically. He is a world beater. Face it, he's where you're not. He'll crook his little finger and you'll come running like a little bimbo. Not for you, babe. What kind of a romance is this? Don't be naïve!"

"Loren," Summer said sharply, "I don't know anything, and you know less, so cool it." But she did know. She wanted Roger but had no idea where this was going. "I only know he is the first man I've been interested in, in a damn long time."

The waiter and a busboy hovered close to their table, peering at them, water pitcher at the ready. It was an LA thing.

"I have to let this play itself out, Loren, and if I'm wrong and I get shot down, it will be finished. It will be my poker game—maybe I could have a busted flush. In the meantime, I still go out on dates."

"Right!" Loren guffawed. "I can count on one hand all your big dates. Puss, I just don't want you to be another notch on his silver Santa Fe belt. I would guess."

Summer reached for Loren's hand across the table

and squeezed. "I appreciate you want to spare me pain, but maybe I need to take this leap. Give me a little space."

Summer withdrew her hand and toyed with her Chinese chicken salad, eyes downcast, not wanting to meet Loren's gaze. She feared her best friend was right on. Hope springs eternal. *Right. Damn him, and damn his eyes.*

"Works for me." Loren shook her hands in the air, miming *Okay, I give up.* She chewed silently and studied her gorgeous and talented friend, thinking Summer could have any guy she wanted. She needed Roger Medvey like a hole in the head. Loren admired her friend's guts and courage, supposing it came from her father's side. She couldn't help but wonder what kind of woman her mother had been.

"Well, you can count on me. I won't fix you up with anyone who's just out of rehab, or been married more than three times. Why not come out and troll the nightclubs with me, like maybe . . . tonight? Unless you're waiting by the phone for the M-man to call?" Loren quickly amended, "Ladybug, sorry, I couldn't resist that dig."

Summer gave her a sour smirk and cocked her head to the side. "What are you doing, taking a survey? Loren, you're great. I have my trusty computer and the sequel to keep me occupied. This is not exactly pining away. Look at me, does this look like pining?"

The waiter crowded their table ready to refill the water glasses that were three-quarters full. They had their own little El Niño going on.

When lunch was over, Loren grabbed for the check. "Split it, wanna put it on a card?"

Summer had her Visa ready to pay.

"It's been swell. I gotta fly." Loren stood up, one foot already out the door.

Summer waved her away. "Go on, I'll take it. I owe you a ton."

They parted, giving each other the Hollywood past-each-cheek kiss. Loren went off to a recording session. She had been toying with recording a duet with her father, from one of his classic hits. He might be dead, but he was still the most-played recording artist ever, and probably always would be. With new technology, everything was possible. Loren Palmer had so much talent, Summer told her over and again. It was time she used it.

Chapter Twelve

Summer attended endless meetings regarding her "hot property," as the trades were referring to *The Pirate and the Lady*, calling her the bright light on filmmaking's horizon. Whatever that meant.

Solley included Summer in all meetings involving the pitch of the script. He was amazed at how quickly she could sit in a room with powerful men like Eisner or Katzenberg and have the guts to disagree about how her movie should be made. Before long, she was invading the good old boys club and had been accepted as one of them, in an industry where that was no easy thing.

Overnight, she learned how to walk the walk and talk the talk. Watching Solley wheel and deal was poetry in motion; Summer felt his delivery was perfection. When making his pitch, he would wait a beat to prolong the suspense. You had to hang on his every word, and he spoke so softly they would lean in straining to catch every word.

Solley was profoundly proud whenever Summer

was perfectly comfortable voicing her own strong and sometimes different opinions in deference to a room full of some of the most powerful men, who were used to little or no resistance to their ideas from anyone. She had them wetting their lips in anticipation, waiting for her next plumb suggestion. Solley sat in awe of her innate abilities, watching her like the cat who swallowed the canary. She employed just the right balance by playing the right cards, getting them out on the table, and above all, being feminine. Things were moving so quickly her personal life was put on hold, and yet Roger Medvey invaded her thoughts constantly.

After weeks went by with no telephone call or note, Summer chalked her experience with him up to a Big Huge Mistake. The hole in her heart was the size of a grapefruit. He simply had to be the sharpest con artist Summer had ever encountered. It hurt! She would cross the street to avoid him. Summer realized Loren was one smart cookie, and she should have listened to her friend.

His picture appeared on the society page with Carole Titian again at his side, attending a charity ball in Pasadena. He had been in town and had not even called her! *Why?* she wondered. And the why of it drove her crazy.

Solley Lester arranged for a meeting at New Line Productions. "There are new people in charge since my last pitch," he told her. "Keep your fingers crossed."

Within days, all hell broke loose. *The Pirate and the Lady* became a hot script, causing an adrenaline rush in Hollywood boardrooms that initiated ritual bidding wars. Suddenly, two production companies wanted it. Two! It left Summer too breathless to think about it. Suddenly everyone was her new best friend, and Summer Murphy was the flavor of the month. They were talking directors for her screenplay like Scorsese or Adrian Lyne. There were others, like Mike Figgis and Neil Jordan, who were also expressing interest in her project. Somehow the trades printed information about her, and wild rumors persisted daily.

"I don't want you to be a Nervous Nelly, Sum, it's a wild card. Suddenly the market has a certain open-mindedness. Westerns and period romances aren't taboo. They can get made," Solley said.

"It's all happening too fast for me to be nervous. I saw my name in the *Reporter*. 'Who is that girl?' I wondered. Working on the sequel is the only way for me to stay sane."

He slid right into his question about Medvey. "Did you ever hear from Roger?" Solley winced in a mock *I told you so*.

"Solley, don't go there. Nothing good can come of it."

"I'm flummoxed. Roger is simply the smartest, sharpest person; he wouldn't stay away unless he had a good reason. Give him a chance, Sum. Things are not always what they appear."

"As far as I'm concerned, Mr. Super Mogul has a narcissistic personality disorder. He's totally wrapped up in himself. I don't want to discuss him, Solley." She was angry beyond all reason. "If I never see him again it will be too soon."

"So you don't care at all?"

"Didn't you tell me to answer 'No comment' if I were questioned about my private life, Broker-Meister?"

"For a shiksa, you're pretty bright." Solley gave Summer a rare hug. She liked to put on a tough front, but he knew better. In a soft tone, he said, "The lady protest too much." He certainly thought she did.

* * *

"The adrenaline rush was premature. None of the companies courting us closed a deal," Summer bitched to Loren on the phone late one night.

"In Hollywood, it's called hurry up and wait," Loren said.

"As an unknown writer," Summer said, "this is going to kill me. Up one day, down the next. The thrills have turned into anxiety. It's not any fun. As a matter of fact, it's hell.

"Several companies wanted to option but haven't. Solley's a rock; he tells me this is par for the course in Hollywood, that I should get used to the sublime and the absurd.

"He says when we get a director everything else will fall into place, but I'm too tired to think about it. Good night, Gracie."

* * *

After several disappointments, one right after another, Solley took the project to Ted Turner's company. Summer was beginning to lose heart. Solley explained that projects don't often end up where they start out in Hollywood and told her to just hang tough. He said, "Michael Douglas's *One Flew Over the Cuckoo's Nest* took ten years in turnaround."

Summer groaned. "Not a comfort, Solley. Tell me *The Pirate* isn't going to take that long. I will be in my thirties, an old lady in Hollywood—their standard, not mine."

But then it all came together so quickly. Turner picked up the option of *The Pirate and the Lady* in turnaround. He was determined to produce an epic, hers. He was in love with it. It would be a two-picture deal, and it was signed for three million dollars. The news reported it as "an undisclosed amount."

As a first-time writer, it took a long time to let that sink in. Money was no longer or would ever be a problem. She could move, have her own bathroom. If only her dad could share this with her. Maybe he was?

"You see, my dear, when one producer gets off the bandwagon, another gets on. Voila, turnaround!" Solley grinned triumphantly.

Sal Turmino reconsidered and signed on as director. He was coming off two action thrillers and was eager to try his hand at historical romance. The cast was stellar: Jeff Bridges and Sigourney Weaver, with Morgan Freeman as the wise chief who is rescued by the privateer, Captain Patrick O'Brien.

Eight weeks had now passed since Summer had heard from Roger Medvey. Their brief romance replayed hundreds of times in her head. She shrugged miserably. She wasn't the same person who had flung herself at him two months ago. By now he must have read and heard about the sale of her script. She could admit only to herself that she was in love with a man who had simply used her. She had been blissed out for a quick few days. Thinking about it made her become unglued. It embarrassed her.

It had been a fantasy for sure, one she had dreamed of and never counted on happening.

Chapter Thirteen

Summer found a tiny, cozy wood-frame house in Laurel Canyon, a wooded haven off the Sunset Strip that fooled her into thinking she was in the country. At last she would have a bathroom to herself. She would try her hand at gardening. Nothing ever grew in the desert, and she loved living things. Emma had helped her find the rustic house.

She'd been wonderful to Summer ever since she came to Hollywood. Because of Summer's affection for the woman, the decision to leave the boarding house had been put off until finally Emma brought it up and suggested she get a place of her own. It became their inside joke that she had hit the lottery and could be Miss Rich Bitch, and was! Preparations were made for Summer to move, and Emma was sad but glad for her.

* * *

"Phone, dearie." Emma tapped hard on the bathroom door. Summer came out wearing a towel wrapped around her head turban style. Emma never got tired of looking at the beautiful young woman, the child she never had.

"Thanks, Emma." Summer took the phone and said in a low pleasant voice, "Hello."

"It's Roger."

She took a deep breath and, with as much sarcasm as the law allowed, said, "Roger who?"

"Come on, Summer, I want to see you, to explain," he said.

"You think you owe me an explanation? I don't have the time," she replied impatiently. "I'm in the middle of packing right now.

On second thought," she added, "I share an office with Solley. I could see you there at the Institute."

"Wherever you say," Roger answered quickly. He was neither condescending nor timid.

Summer could hardly think straight. His voice was balm on her ears. Her palms were moist and her heart beat double time. The silence was deafening; neither he nor she spoke for what seemed an eternity.

"Wherever, whenever you feel most comfortable," Roger murmured.

"Four o'clock? The office is in the basement."

"I have visited Mr. Lester, I will find you. Sir Galahad is on the way."

She hung the receiver up and leaned her forehead against the wall, tears stinging her eyes. The office was neutral territory. She wouldn't let him pull any shenanigans. What could he possibly offer as explanation for disappearing from her life?

Summer chose a pair of jeans and an oversized Turner Entertainment T-shirt. But after changing her clothes several times, she put on a frothy little Chico's outfit.

Roger was waiting for her when she came to open the office. They surveyed each other. He looked just a bit uncomfortable.

Summer offered him the most uncomfortable chair across from the desk. She bolted behind the desk, placing herself as far away as she could in the tiny space.

"You wanted to talk, so talk!" Her arms were folded tight across her chest as a defense mechanism. Roger looked gorgeous to her, even more so than she remembered.

"There is every reason and no reason why you should be upset with me." He started not hesitantly but boldly without excuse.

"Speak in English, please. My patience is at a low ebb," Summer bristled. "If you expected a welcome, think again." She closed her eyes in exasperation. "I suggest you take your little act on the road somewhere else. I'm not amused."

She looked at her watch. "Let's have it." Summer gave no quarter; her body language told Roger how annoyed she was. "I'm waiting," she dared.

"You eradicated me from your life, no contact, at

all, no phone call or letters. Surely there was some way to get a message to me," she snapped.

Out of control, Summer spewed out the rest of her complaints. Roger listened patiently as her rage ran the gambit.

She listed them one by one: "You were never going to let me go now that you found me. What was that all about?" She gave him no way to respond, venting until some of her anger was spent. Then she stopped her tirade long enough for Roger to get a word in edgeways.

Her recriminations of his self-serving ego and maniacal behavior were how she perceived him. A no-account womanizing bastard—a user. Yet he could still see in her eyes a look reflecting her anger, hate, and love.

"There was no way to see you or call you. I was being advised by my battery of lawyers. It was for your protection," Roger admitted. "I wanted to with all of my soul. I did!"

"Did you?" Summer pulled a wry face, too confused to comment. Leaning toward, Roger she sought his eyes to see if he was sincere. She gave him a slow, insolent smile, daring him to go on. "Yes?"

"My life was in danger, as were those close to me. I was being stalked. Dangerously stalked."

"You expect me to believe that?" She looked at him suspiciously. "What about all the benefits and business meetings, the ladies on your arm? The press is always with you." She was spoiling for a fight.

"The man who threatened me and my family would have threatened you, too, if he could get to you. Fortunately he did not know about us. He tried to hurt Carole—there was an incident with her car, I forget the details. Not important. I got her a bodyguard."

"This *is* true?" She was incredulous. She turned away to put some space between them.

It worried Roger that she refused to believe him. He was persistent that she should, and he would go to any length.

"Sweetheart, I didn't want to worry about anyone attacking you. The week after the gala in Santa Fe, the man was caught outside my home. He had duct tape, handcuffs, and guns when they found him. He was threatening to kidnap me and possibly my loved ones. Sending weird letters was the beginning of it. I didn't want to overreact at first, but then there was a series of strange incidents on the ranch. Cattle poisoned, a fire in the tack house. Summer, please."

He pulled her around to face him. "Look at me, please!" Roger went on. "Luckily I was out of town when they caught him. We have had an indictment, and he is in jail awaiting trial. At my request I was listed as John Doe in the court papers. With some fancy legal maneuvering, the judge agreed to delete my name, and he imposed a gag order on the attorneys, plaintiff, and defendant. The press never made the connection. That way *Hard Copy* and other television tabloids couldn't make everything ten times worse."

He hung his head, too exhausted to continue. He looked drained. His face was a map of hurt. Tears clearly showed in his eyes.

"You're serious!" Summer's mouth was dry as wadded cotton, her hands shaking and her heart beating very fast as the thought of the danger to Roger registered.

All of her anger toward him turned to amazement, sympathy, and understanding. "You could have told me, I . . . I didn't know what to think, I—" Summer realized he had been protecting her, and that brought an avalanche of tears. "Who is this man? Where is he now?"

Roger walked around the desk and lifted her into his arms. "Shh, don't you cry. He's in jail awaiting trial. He can't hurt either one of us now. I'm here now, and I want us to be together. I love you." He patted her hair and pressed a trail of kisses to her face. He wiped the falling tears from her eyes with his fingers.

Reaching into his coat pocket, he withdrew a handkerchief and put it into her hand. "I wanted to be sure he was locked away. I couldn't feel you would be safe if he knew about us. Until that was a fact." He could not go on; he was too drained.

"What you must have gone through." She sighed and her lips curved to a smile. "Poor Roger! I know, I read about this case in the paper. It was a guessing game for the gossip-mongers. I never dreamt . . . it could be you."

"Stalkers have amazing cunning and can be as dangerous as terrorists. Sweetheart, I've never been paranoid, but this incident made a believer out of me. I was told to stay away from you, have no contact. That was hell for me."

Summer felt as if a jolt of electricity passed through her body. "Roger, I . . ." Her eyes came up to meet his dark-blue ones, smoldering with passion.

"I knew I had been followed around the country. In several cities I had this uncanny, eerie feeling. I told the police in LA, as well as New Mexico. I suspected the stalker planned to make his kidnap attempt from the Lazzara, if he failed in Santa Fe, since there was less security than at my home. They captured him on a night when we had a double enter the ship in my place. This is where it gets nastier. Facing him in the courtroom was a horror. Carole, unfortunately, had to appear." He noticed that Summer's lips were quivering. He stopped talking, took her in his arms, and kissed her long and hard.

Solley Lester entered the room, preoccupied with his own thoughts, and stopped short, seeing them in an embrace. He started to do an immediate about-face when Roger reached across the desk and stopped him. "Stay!"

"The errant person returns," Solley said, trying to make light of the moment, but couldn't help see Summer's tear-stained face. "What . . . why all the tears? God, I hate mysteries."

"Come on, Solley, let's have some lunch and we'll tell you about it." Roger put on his most amiable smile. He had his arm around Summer and she leaned into him.

"Sure," Solley said. "What meshuggaas is this who's paying?"

Summer and Roger couldn't resist the good fortune of having another person to tell their problems to.

* * *

The paparazzi had a field day shooting stills of Roger Medvey and Summer Murphy wherever they were. She was the hot ticket, the toast of the town; he, the movie mogul with the Midas touch.

Screenwriter Summer Murphy, whose face and fig-ure made love to the camera, was a prime target. Her film, *The Pirate and the Lady*, had garnered respect, praise, and awards. For the past few months, the press screamed for photos wherever she went. Summer was sure anonymity wouldn't be hers for a long time, if ever again.

They were on their way to the Academy Awards, and she had a nomination for Best Original Screen-play, among others. "This way, Summer, over here!

Turn just one little bit, over here!" Summer was now in the middle of a chorus of voices over the din of the crowd.

"Roger, give us those pearly whites, over here, over here! Yes, sir." There were those photos taken with zoom lenses, some not so flattering.

Roger and Summer obliged the photographers with broad, rehearsed smiles whenever they were able, and the crowds ate it up. They went wild around them.

Roger told her under his breath, "Now you see why I watch the Academy Awards on television. You can see it much better than in the fray. It is nothing but a backslapping cleavage parade. Smile, Baby June," he joked.

He made sure to hold on to her arm. A storm had swept the Southern California coast and dumped a full four inches in six hours. Summer walked cautiously down the red-carpeted entry that was puckered and soggy in places. She was part of and surrounded by familiar, famous faces. She was beginning to take for granted those celebrities known the world over, and they were all smiling at them. At her. This was Tinsel Town, and she was now in the upper strata. This excitement brought back the memory of tending bar less than two years ago. It left her feeling giddy. The gown she wore and the jewels from Tiffany's were on loan for the night. They walked toward the auditorium of the Dorothy Chandler Pavilion and were corralled by comedian Joan Rivers and her daughter, Melissa, for an interview. There was only time for a quick sound bite from each of them.

Joan asked, "Who is your designer and how did you pick this particular dress, Summer Murphy?" Joan extended a welcoming hand. "How does it feel to have a nomination for your first film?"

"The dress is Naeem Khan, a new and exciting young designer. What can I say, just being nominated would surely be enough to win . . . I can't hope. I'm in some great company."

"Tell the audience where this exquisite jewelry is from. Would you be the person responsible for the rubies and diamonds, Roger?"

"It would be my pleasure to deck this beautiful woman with gems, but she is an independent woman. She won't let me."

"Oh, oh, oh!" Joan clutched her throat. "Summer, I know you could buy your own gems now with your sequel in production." To the audience she said, "This young lady is rich, rich, rich. Can we talk? But don't ruin it for the rest of us. Accept a few carats now and again, I always say." She laughed.

As if on cue, Melissa took over. They were mother and daughter, and very good together. She asked, "Roger, are you nervous for her?"

Roger knew the drill and was prepared with his statements. He smiled his most winsome smile and made a little quarter turn, favoring the camera. "Just . . . we'll wait and see."

Joan said, "Good luck, Summer." She smiled a knowing smile. "I saw *The Pirate and the Lady* three times, had a good cry."

"Can't wait for the sequel," Melissa added.

They moved on to ABC's coverage area and reiterated the same questions like good sports.

Roger steered Summer out of the clamoring crowd and into the lines of people entering the auditorium to await the opening of the envelopes for the 1999 Academy Awards. Roger could feel the tension in Summer's arm, and he held her somewhat more firmly, to let her know she was protected. They were grateful when they reached their aisle seats close to the stage. The walk down the aisle had seemed never-ending. Summer let out a long sigh and settled in. The Best Original Screenplay category always came late in the evening. She felt like she was floating. Solley had told her not to be farmisht, but that only made her more nervous.

Billy Crystal, emceeing on stage, mentioned the hundreds of millions of people tuned in to the broadcast. It was the most elaborate television production, with numbers performed by stars of the highest caliber. It was unnerving. Unbelievable. How Summer wished her father were here to see this. Her claws were now firmly in place on the fleeing animal called success.

Still, with any luck Billy Crystal would relax her with his antics, to get her through this night. Roger's warm hand holding hers gave her a feeling of reverie.

All those associated with the production of *The Pirate and the Lady* were seated together in the front rows of the auditorium. There was a constant barrage of back-slapping and thumbs-ups. Potential winners were always seated up front, for a shorter trip to the stage should they be one of the winners.

Her picture had won the People's Choice Award, the Foreign Press Award, and the Golden Globe. Scuttlebutt around town was that the writer and director awards should be a shoo-in. They had racked up nine other awards in various categories, among them Best Supporting Actor and Best Supporting Actress.

It seemed surreal to Summer to be sitting in the audience with the esteemed stars of show business. Tom Hanks and his beautiful and talented wife, Rita Wilson, came in and sat down in the middle of the same row they were in, giving a thumbs-up to Roger and Summer. Goldie Hawn could be heard giggling about something in that inimitable Goldie way.

Turner Entertainment had signed a three-picture deal with Summer just the past week, and the industry was chewing on that. The new kid on the block was now one of them, and as is tradition in show biz, they loved her. *Variety* and *Reporter* stayed tuned for her every move. She would be busy until 2004.

As the lights dimmed, Summer had a million thoughts spinning in her head. The opening number was a gorgeous extravaganza of dancers dancing the tango dressed in brilliantly colored Argentine costumes, from the picture *Tango Style*. Summer sat with her back to the up-and-coming director William Galen. He leaned forward in his seat and tapped her shoulder. In a stage whisper he said, "Someday we will work together."

Summer turned and gave him a wide, appreciative smile. Her heart was beating so fast, she ordered it to behave. Roger gave her arm a pat and let her know he was there for her.

To the outside world, she was a poised and confident woman. Inside, she was a frightened beginner who had dared them to find her out. She was, after all, just a kid from the arid desert. When she read about the grosses of pictures in the trades, they had always seemed like Monopoly money to her. *The Pirate and the Lady* had grossed $350 million, and that was domestic. The futures from the foreign market, cable, and video promised to double that. That made Summer now a bankable writer. And Sal Turmino, the director, was now a bankable director. Everyone was clamoring for them, the whole shebang, for future projects.

Solley simply said, as if it was ordained, "How fortuitously it has all turned out." Summer joked that he was referring to his 15 percent commission on the sale of her screenplay, though she knew differently. Solley had become much more than an agent. He was teacher, a mentor, and she loved him as a daughter would.

* * *

It was down the stretch to the close of the evening. *The Pirate and the Lady* had gathered the top nominations in Costume, Special Effects, Original Screenplay, Editing, and Art Direction. The Best Actor and Actress awards were always saved for next to last. *The Pirate and the Lady* had been nominated in those categories, but they had lost in the Supporting Actor and Actress categories. Summer felt bad for the performers, who had given stellar performances. Roger had to admit there was no rhyme or reason. "In La La Land," he said, "go with the flow."

The pundits were surprised, as the odds in Las Vegas had clearly pointed to a win that went much deeper than the five they finally won. Summer was breathless that the film had gotten so much attention.

Behind the scenes, backstage television crews from every network were clamoring to speak to each winner. Interviews as they came off stage fresh from their acceptance speeches were immediately broadcast on all the networks. Still photographers were in action, almost like a ballet.

When her name was announced as the winner of

Best Original Screenplay, the world watched as Summer approached the podium. She was the epitome of elegance and understatement. When she delivered her seemingly impromptu acceptance remarks, Hollywood knew they had a new queen. A roar of applause went up for one of their own.

Summer accepted congratulations from presenter Mike Nichols, who said, "That was a hell of chick flick *and* a guy flick, and that ain't easy to do. I've been trying for years." He kissed her, genuinely happy for her win, and handed her the coveted award.

Her speech was dignified and short—she thanked her father and in Gaelic recited the story of the rabbit. She thanked Solley Lester and the Film Institute for being there, and lastly the cast and crew of the production. She smiled at Roger Medvey, calling him "her friend." Summer was succinct.

Now that she was more relaxed, she laughed a delicious throaty laugh and held the statue over her head. "See what you can do when you don't know you're doing it?"

She accepted a roar of laughter from the sophisticated audience, causing Billy Crystal to say, "Hey girl, I tell the jokes!"

She started moving off in the wrong direction, all smiles, not sure if any of this was real. A model onstage redirected her to backstage.

Summer had her first taste of Hollywood hatred directed at her when the actress Lilly Crystal stared her down. They had never been formally introduced, but it was clear that Summer had what Lilly wanted: Roger Medvey. Now she would begin her life in a new strata that was bright as the moon, the sun, and the stars in the sky, but her solid rock would always be Roger. Her man, the one she could count on, and a home in an enchanted place called Santa Fe, New Mexico.

Summer processed the facts. She had done what was not impossible, but improbable. She was her father's daughter. As Irish as a four-leaf clover, and more than that, an independent woman who did not take crap from anyone, but was respectful of those deserving of it.

Summer and Roger married right after that first win. Eight years later, they had twins, named Emma and Ryan. "How Lucky Can a Girl Get?" was the title of the piece she gave with Roger at her side, in a rare interview.

"Writing was the instrument that worked the miracle that made a woman of me," Summer said, in an article appearing in the Sunday Entertainment section of the *New York Times*. The photograph showed a contented writer, wife, and mother. Roger was as proud of her as she was of him.

not THE END

Discussion Questions

1. Summer's mother disappeared before Summer was even three years old. What do you think happened to her?

2. Why is Summer so closed off until meeting Roger Medvey?

3. Who do you think the character of Loren, Summer's best friend, is fashioned after?

4. Is a best friend with good intentions always correct?

5. Where do you think Summer's "nose to the grindstone" work ethic comes from?

6. Does Roger prove to be sincere? How does he show it?

About the Author

A. J. Genis was raised in show business. Her father and mother were both prominent in the motion picture and music businesses. And so A. J. writes what she knows best—show business! *Summer Murphy* is her first novella. Her heroines are all named Summer Murphy in memoriam of her best friend of sixty-five years, who passed away. As an interior designer with the American Society of Interior Designers, she also designed sets for motion pictures and TV. She has written and published multiple articles, stories, and poems.

A. J. has four children and six grandchildren. She enjoys contributing to charitable work for children through the Ronald McDonald House Charities and other nonprofit organizations.